I0717701

SUICIDAL STATE

Sammy endures a traumatic family life starting with her biological mother leaving her in the hands of her father, who was a psychological bully. She is subjected to her father's 5 marriages and one common law wife and the dysfunction that accompanies them. Sammy's brother, his best friend, and two of her stepmothers commit suicide by the time she is in her early twenties.

This book is the story of a toxic relationship that sees Sammy driven to contemplate suicide and homicide.

A must read for anyone trying to understand or survive an abusive parent.

SUICIDAL STATE

SAMMY JO DANCEY

Copyright © 2020 by Sammy Jo Dancey.

ISBN   978-1-970160-24-6 Ebook
tISBN   978-1-970160-24-6 Paperback

All rights reserved. No part of this publication may be reproduced, distributed, or transmitted in any form or by any means, including photocopying, recording, or other electronic or mechanical methods without the prior written permission of the publisher. For permission requests, solicit the publisher via the address below through mail or email with the subject line "Attention: Publication Permission".

This book is based on a true story.

EC Publishing LLC
11100 SW 93rd Court Road, Suite 10-215
Ocala, Florida 34481-5188, USA

Ordering Information:
Quantity sales. Special discounts are available on quantity purchases by corporations, associations, and others. For details, contact the publisher at the address above.

www.ecpublishingllc.com
info@ecpublishingllc.com
+1 (352) 234-6201

Printed in the United States of America

CONTENTS

Chapter One

The Presenting Past

I'm going home. I don't feel well.' Sammy sighed and felt the sharp pain in her head and neck. She looked defiantly at the foreman, expecting the reply he scathingly gave.

'There's nothing wrong with you. I am going to tell your father,' the foreman threatened.

"Oh, just fuck off, you stupid arsehole,' she thought. 'Who the fuck does he think he is? I hate him, I hate my father and his whores, and most of all, I fucking hate this job. Why the fuck did I ever leave the police? I must have been crazy, totally fucking crazy.'

Sammy got into her car, the latest guilt gift from her father stood out due to the private registration number, the 'must have' accessory for life at the family business. She grimaced as she again felt the pain in her head.

'God, I feel ill,' she thought. 'What the hell is happening to me? I can't sleep, I can't eat, I am having panic attacks because I've got so much work to do, not enough time and no support.' The road in front of her seemed a blur. 'Christ Almighty, I just want to block my life out. I can't cope,' Sammy thought as she began to cry.

As Oxleys Hall appeared on the horizon, she thought about how beautiful it was. The old Hall was stunning, set in picturesque countryside in a lonely green field. She had heard rumours of it being haunted but had laughed them off. If she was anything, it was a realist. Lionel was there to greet her, his black coat shining in the September sun, his perfect green eyes smiling up at her; he loyally followed her out of the car, across the wall, and up to the house. Hoping she had got some cat food in for him, she opened the door.

How could she explain what was happening to her father? He would never understand and would be furious with her for having time off. The company was at a critical time for growth. She felt as though she was letting everybody down. The kettle began to boil as she collapsed in a heap on the kitchen floor, crying. Sammy was twenty-seven years old and single; it was rare for anyone to do anything for her. She did delegate, but being groomed for succession of the family business was not something she could delegate. She went upstairs to change out of her suit and into her jeans. 'I hate suits. I am not a suit person,' she muttered to herself. She picked her mobile up and called the doctor. The appointment was made for the following morning. '"Oh god, what am I going to say to the doctor? He is going to think I am crazy too. What's going on in my head? Am I being haunted? Is this place haunted?' her mind began to regress. What was going on? Was she having the breakdown that so many people had warned her about?

Sammy's biological mother's name was Molly. Sammy's brother, was four years older than her. Her father separated from Molly when Sammy was just eighteen months old, but she stayed living with her father and brother, not remembering ever living with her mother as she had left when Sammy was at such an early age. There had been cruel comments from aunts that Molly had left Sammy in her pram at the shops and ran off. Sammy became a master at selective hearing.

Chrissie was her father's second wife. She was the person whom she looked upon as her mother. They moved in with her first stepmom and her daughter Kathy when she was eighteen months. Sammy recalled that Number Two married her father when she was eight years old. Since her brothers and first stepmothers' deaths, Sammy had trouble remembering anything much about them. Why couldn't she remember her childhood? She had successfully shut years out of her memory. Trauma that was too painful to remember.

She did see her biological mother and her partner once a fortnight on a Sunday up until she was sixteen. Her biological mother's partner was an ex-employee of her fathers. He had two children whom he had left with his ex-wife to run away with her biological mother. Sammy thought they were both irresponsible, selfish bastards. She found it difficult as a child as divorce was uncommon, feeling like the odd one out with her friends. They were all bemused by her calling her stepmom 'Mom' and her biological mom 'Mom'. It was confusing. Her father suggested she call them by numbers to make it easier, so Molly became 'Number One' and Chrissie became 'Number Two'.

There was always underlying animosity between Number One and Number Two, so she chose her words carefully not to upset either party. She felt like she was a pawn in their games. She also felt very sad and wished her parents were together like her friends' parents were. The two women were poles apart. Number One being of average intellect, and lower class, she worked in a dead-end job in a factory and seemed very dissatisfied with life. Over the years, Sammy had nicknamed her and her partner 'Doom and Gloom'. She did not drive and did not appear to have any ambition. On the other hand, Number Two was full of life, motivated, intelligent, extremely sociable, and a former dancer. She ran her own company, drove a sports car, and holidayed in St Tropez. She also had a motor cruiser in Puerto Banús, where Sammy had often holidayed.

Her father never spoke about Number One, but it was obvious that he hated her. Sammy did not bond with her as she was never in her company long enough and had already bonded with Number Two, a very natural reaction for an eighteen-month-old baby. Sammy knew this was apparent to Number One, who would always try to make Sammy feel guilty if she called Number Two 'Mom'. Number One would play the part of the victim to Oscar nomination level, wallowing in her guilt-mongering, whining that she could never live up to Number Two in terms of wealth or intelligence.

Sammy was not a happy child and was always aware that Number Two was not her actual mother. Her brother was quiet and seemed sad. The relationship between her brother, stepsister, and Sammy was one of forced compliance and good behavior. There were often fights between her brother and stepsister, and her stepsister was often jealous of Sammy's time with Number Two, who wasn't Sammy's 'real mom', as she often reminded her. Her stepsister let her jealousy out by bullying Sammy and assaulting her. On one occasion, she broke her nose and blackened her eyes after dragging her down the stairs by her hair. Sammy would try to escape from the house as much as she could by going to the local park. She also ran away when she was ten but was found and dragged home.

Sammy's father was very controlling and would demand cooperation and a neat and orderly home. He wanted his children to be compliant. One of his favourite sayings was 'Children should be seen but not heard.' He would often encourage competition between the children and introduced bribes such as money and chocolate if they played his games. Punishment was swift and unforgiving; he used a dog lead to beat them. A sense of fear lingered in the family home.

Sammy shuddered as the distant haunting memories returned and felt icily cold. Lionel startled her as he jumped into her lap. She stroked him and tried to switch off her mind, but vivid memories came hurtling out of her past.

It was the summer when she was eleven years old; her father was in a rage after they had dinner. It was usual practice for Number Two to cook, her stepsister to wash up, her brother to dry, and Sammy to put away the dishes. Number Two suggested that evening that her father should do it and give all of the kids a break. He flew into a rage; his language turned the air blue as he smashed every item of crockery on the patio outside shouting, 'I rule this house. I am the man. I pay all the bills. You fucking do it!' His face turned red contorted with rage; his eyes were cold and evil. Sammy could see the image of herself as a young girl running upstairs in terror and hiding under her bed.

The second incident was late at night. She could hear her father calling Number Two names, and she heard her begging him to stop. 'Is his greasy cock bigger than mine, you whore? Is he better at fucking you than me? Do you like the feel of his oily cock in your hole?' he bellowed at her.

Sammy got up and walked into their bedroom feigning toothache so as to stop him. He walked out, slamming the door nearly off its hinges. Sammy got into bed with Number Two, trying to protect her. They both sat in silence.

The relationship with her stepsister during the period that her father was married to Number Two was sometimes not very pleasant at all. It was obvious that her stepsister was very unhappy and she did not get along with Sammy's father. As he was the dominant figure in the family, she could not express her unhappiness or discomfort towards him. She picked on Sammy instead as she was five years younger and an easy target.

There were many fights, and Sammy used to try and avoid her stepsister as much as possible. The school holidays were the worst times as her stepsister used to bully her. She felt as though she lived in a real-life version of Cinderella. If Sammy did not cooperate she would be assaulted. Up until Sammy was about twelve, she took the abuse and assaults. However, during the summer holidays, her stepsister attacked her for refusing to wash up after her and her boyfriend. Sammy fought back and fought back hard, slamming her fingers in the door screaming, 'Don't you ever touch me again!' Sammy slammed her stepsisters' fingers in the door hinge and shut the door on them. They fractured and she never dared assault her again.

Sammy heard the shrill of the telephone that jolted her back to the present. Looking at the clock, she was shocked to see it was 7 p.m.

'Hi, Sammy,' said a friendly voice, 'just wondered how you are?' Becky, the receptionist from work, enquired.

'Hey, I feel awful, think its tonsillitis,' Sammy lied. She was a director and still had to maintain her professionalism. She couldn't possibly tell the staff what was really happening. 'I am going to the doctor's tomorrow morning. When William calls work, tell him I am ill, will you, please?' Sammy knew that he wouldn't call her at home, just the office. After all, that's all she was to him—an employee to be used and worn out. Walking up the stairs, Sammy shivered as though someone had walked across her grave. The wind was picking up, and it howled through the field. It was so dark at night at the Hall. As the days grew shorter and she spent her first autumn there, she had to admit it was getting a little spooky. Climbing into bed, she thought how enormous and empty the house was—far too big for her on her own, but then again, it looked good for the business.

Sammy could not help thinking about her past; it was in her every waking thought lately. She remembered that Number Two used to cut her hair so short it made her cry. As a result, Sammy looked like a boy for most of her pre-teens. Number One would comment when she visited that she wanted to wash and style Sammy's hair; this made her uncomfortable as it made her feel like some sort of doll. She did not want to be picked up and played with for a couple of hours by her biological mother. She wasn't a part-time interest—she was a person with feelings. Nor indeed did she want to endure vile haircuts from Number Two. The whole situation made her very sad; she had never considered herself in the least attractive. She was never told by her stepsister or stepmother that she was pretty or good in any way. She enviously noticed the way other mothers lavished praise and adoration on their daughters, but she didn't receive any. Sammy felt unloved and like there was something terribly wrong with her. A smile was something foreign to her.

At thirteen, she learnt that Number Two was having an affair with her business partner and that her father was having an affair with his secretary. Her father did not speak to her about it. She was told on a Saturday afternoon by her stepmom, who had packed her father's, brothers, and her belongings into suitcases and left them at the door. Sammy was moved from her home and school without warning. She was shocked, heartbroken, and very unhappy but complied as usual. The wrath of her father was a powerful inhibitor. After they separated from Number Two, her contact with her stepsister was virtually non-existent. Number Two remained at their family home and moved her lover in with her. Her stepsister moved to Somerset. Her family had been shattered and splintered beyond repair. Life as she knew it would never be the same.

Her father's lover was introduced to her and her brother on the same day that they left what had been their family home. Sammy was ambivalent.

They moved into a house that her father had bought for them all with her two young children, Justin and Emily. Justin was a year or so younger than Sammy, and Emily was five or six years younger. Her father's lover became 'Number Three'. Her father designated bedrooms for the children and then went to work. His strict domineering demeanor was constant; he was never kind or affectionate and always demanded compliance. It was a shock being forced to live in a house with three complete strangers and, even more so, having to share a bedroom with a girl she had never met before. It was clear that Justin and Emily were also distressed by their newly imposed circumstances. Justin and her brother shared a bedroom. Her brother was becoming more distant. He drove at the time and did not spend a lot of time in the house at all. Sammy disengaged from the new life totally. She looked after herself and spent most of her spare time in the youth center. She also took an evening and weekend job, not spending much time with Number Three or her children's company. It seemed like a joke.

The relationship between Number Three and her father was not working, and after about a year of squabbles and embarrassing scenes, she moved out. Her father bought her and her children a house about half a mile away on the same road, and they moved into that property. Sammy never saw her brother and his father bond; they hardly ever spoke to one another, and her brother seemed morose. They did not have a loving relationship, and her father seemed strangely hostile towards his own children.

Sammy's tears returned as she looked back through the years. The memories were painful; the emptiness she was feeling was overwhelming. She turned the hot tap on, poured bubble bath in the bath, and undressed. She unexpectedly felt like she was not alone. She looked around rapidly but saw nothing. She felt a presence. She could swear she was being watched. A shiver tingled her spine, and the hairs on the back of her neck stood up. Her eyes grew larger, and adrenaline surged through her body. Trying to remain calm and rational, she immersed herself into the bath.

The warm, scented water soothed her nerves as she told herself to calm down. 'I must stop thinking about the past. It's making me jittery.'

She scolded herself for being so utterly ridiculous. As she relaxed listening to K. D. Lang, she thought about her doctor's appointment and what she was going to say. There was a conversation she didn't relish having. Drying herself and smoothing on rich moisturizing lotion, she got into her big comfy double bed. Pulling the covers over her, she snuggled into bed and drifted off to sleep. Out of the blue, she heard footsteps on the wooden floor. She felt the bed move. The mattress moved downwards as though someone had climbed into bed next to her, but there was no one there—she was alone. She froze. She couldn't move. She wanted to scream but couldn't. She was completely immobilised. She felt an arm wrap around her and a leg wrap itself across her thigh and then heard a voice, 'This is beautiful, Sammy. Everything is going to be fine.'

As suddenly as the presence came, it went, leaving her in such a state of panic she couldn't breathe. Her heart was pounding, and she was sweating with fear and disbelief.

'Oh my god! What was that?! What happened then?! Who on earth or what on earth was that?!' She tried to rationalize. She tried to stem the enormous tingles up her nose and down her spine. 'Was that her brother? That must have been her brother. Oh my god, oh my god, oh my god!'

Her heart had leapt into her mouth. She was convinced at that minute in time that her brother's spirit had come to her. But why? How could that be possible? Was she hallucinating? Dreaming? Or was that real? Was what she had dared to believe in all her life but not had the guts to accept actually possible? Had she connected with a spirit? She sat exasperated on the edge of her bed, shaking, frightened, eyes open wide, staring at the door. She was taken back to the time when he was alive, when she had been happy, before his death had ripped all the joy out of her soul.

She had adored her big brother. He used to call her his 'little princess' and seemed to intuitively know that she was sad about their family situation. It was a sadness that they shared although it was unspoken. Sammy saw him as her best friend and confidant, the man who would always protect her. She had loved him very much, and in her world of chaos, mixed emotions, and unidentified feelings, he was her rock to lean on. She often felt it was just her and him against the world and that their father was a dominant, cold-hearted, evil bastard, who would scare them both to death with his rages and broody silent treatment. Her brother was her place of love and comfort, someone who understood how she felt. She did not know of any other children of divorcees apart from those her father brought into their lives, and they had both therefore found it hard to deal with. By the ages of thirteen and nineteen, respectively, they had experienced three mother figures, all of whom appeared to have their own neuroses and hidden agendas. Her brother was the only person in the world that she could be herself with. They had taken dance lessons together and had won medals for Latin American and ballroom dancing. Sammy used to ride on the back of his motorbike, and when he passed his driving test, he used to ferry her and her friends around. He was the first to defend her, make her smile, and help her through her difficult teenage emotions; growing up was hard enough without all the additional dramas they had to cope with. They had been very close.

It was September twelve years previously when her brother drove up to the house in his car. He seemed moody and distracted as he walked up the stairs and passed Sammy's bedroom. 'Hi,' said Sammy. 'What's up?' Her brother grunted something under his breath. She did not take much notice, but as he walked past again on the way down, she said. 'See ya.' He ignored her. Being sarcastic, she quipped, 'Love you too!' as the front door closed behind him on a cold, grey autumn day. The following morning, she heard someone knocking officially at the door. She opened it to a young policewoman.

'Can I help you? What's wrong?' she questioned. She was alone as her father was at work.

'Does anyone own a Ford Capri?' the police officer asked.

'My brother, does. Why? What's wrong?' Sammy began to panic, her hands began to tremble, and she felt faint. She was in her nightshirt at the time as the knocking at the door had got her out of bed.

'We have found a dead body in the car, a young man in his teens. There is also a note on a beer mat saying, "Sorry, Sammy. I love you." Are you Sammy? Could it be your brother in the car?'

'Yes,' she replied.

'We need someone to come to the morgue and identify the body. Are you alone?' The police officer looked grave.

'Yes,' the worlds barely passed out of her mouth. 'I better find my father.' With her head spinning and hardly able to walk, she managed to get upstairs and get dressed. Still in shock, she got into the police car and directed the officer to her father's place of business. As she walked to the office door with the police officer, her legs were giving way. She had a terrible piercing noise in her head and was fighting to hold back the scream she so desperately wanted to release out of her mouth.

She could see the police officer talking to her father but could not hear any words. It felt like she was in slow motion and the world had stopped moving. The noise in her head was deafening. She was totally mortified.

Sitting bolt upright in bed, Sammy breathed deeply. Had she been dreaming? Was she still asleep? 'That must have been a dream,' she thought. She needed to wash her face and calm herself. As she walked into the en suite bathroom, she couldn't believe her eyes. The bath was covered in faeces; it was splattered everywhere. She gagged on the smell and looked for Lionel; he had never defecated in the house before, not ever. 'Oh, Jesus,' she thought, 'what's going on?' Sammy cleaned up the mess and got in the shower. Again she felt something. She couldn't quite put her finger on it, but the shiver up her spine and the tingle in her nose were telling her she was not alone. Lionel walked into the en suite and started to scratch at the shower panel, his eyes wide and startled, his tail normally stretched out was curling downwards. She turned up the heat and stood still, letting the hot water massage her head. She had a feeling she was not in the shower alone. She couldn't see anyone but felt the presence of someone or something right next to her.

Number Two had identified her brothers' body; she got drunk then and more or less every day for the next ten years. She became unreachable. Her father became even more unreachable, a hard, cold, bitter man, who ignored Sammy and spent his time either with women or gambling. She became invisible to him. Sammy did not receive counselling and went back to school the next day, the first day of the new school term. Number Three came in to school with her and told the headmaster what had happened. Her father did not get involved in this at all. He seemed completely unfazed by the suicide. He never mentioned it and threw himself back into work. The funeral was a nightmare; there were three women all fighting for a place in the funeral car with her father. Number One, Two, and Three were arguing with each other whilst her brother's dead body lay in a coffin outside. Sammy was horrified by the outrageous behavior of these women. Numbness had taken over, and she became withdrawn. She had no indication from her brother that he was suicidal, and the news that he had gassed himself in his car had totally devastated her.

As the flashback left her mind, she got out of the shower. She thought how she now could not recall much else about her brother or the funeral or her own personal life, as from that moment, she had shut down emotionally. She had blocked it out, put a smile on her face, and carried on living an unemotional life. To the outsider, she appeared determined, strong, and independent. She had changed utterly and instantaneously on the third day of September as the autumn leaves began to fall. Her heart was totally and completely broken. She did not cry, she did not talk about it, she never opened her mouth; she locked it deep inside. She had been in her final year at school when he had committed suicide, and therefore, it was her most important. She struggled to get through the days, and there was an eerie silence in the house. The horrible task of sorting out her brothers 'room and dispensing of his possessions was left to her. The suicide meant that she did not do very well in her exams, and teachers and school friends avoided her, whispering in corners. 'That's her, the girl whose brother has gassed himself.' Sammy wished that she had known and could have stopped him. If only she could have! All she had left was an enormous feeling of guilt. A few weeks after her brother committed suicide, his guilt-ridden best friend killed himself by driving his motorbike into an articulated lorry. Sammy's world was shattered again beyond repair. Two suicides, it was two too many.

She loved her new home; it was a beautiful Grade II listed barn conversion. History stated that it was built in the fifteenth century and had been a hall with stables and servants' quarters. On further research, Sammy had found that it was supposedly frequented by William Shakespeare and Henry VIII. Stories of orgies and sacrifices had surfaced, and Robert Peel had the original Oxleys Hall burnt down in the eighteenth century. The current Oxleys Hall was the remaining servants' quarters that had been recently converted into twelve mews properties and a central courtyard. The locals still insisted it was haunted, and the local kids used to dare each other to go up there. 'Perhaps there was some truth in the rumors,' she mused; then she remembered the previous night and shrugged it off, concluding that it must have been a dream.

CHAPTER TWO

Depression Surfaces

You have suppressed your childhood traumas and a whole lot more, and it's all coming out, you are depressed and burnt out, Sammy. You are very unstable and vulnerable right now. You need long-term therapy and at least six months off work.' Dr. Hatton smiled gently and genuinely looked concerned. 'So tell me, what happened after your brother's suicide?' he asked.

'In '85, when I was sixteen, my father sold the house and we moved in with Number Three and her children. There were only two bedrooms. Her children's room was partitioned, and I had to sleep in the kitchen on a put-up bed. I was not allowed into the lounge and did not have anywhere to keep all of my belongings; I threw a lot of things away as there just wasn't enough room. My father and Number Three got married sometime after we moved in. I cannot remember the exact date but remember that it was at the registry office. My father's sister thought it would be amusing to make bets with the rest of her family as to how long the marriage would last. Number Three was drinking vodka from a hip flask in the ladies' before the ceremony. She drank a lot, and there was violence in the house afterwards.'

'And how did that make you feel, Sammy?' he questioned.

'Angry and hurt, I guess, like marriage was a big joke.' Sammy looked distraught.

'What happened then?' Dr. Hatton tested.

'I started working at a hotel when I left school. About three months into my time working there, my father turned up with some suitcases and informed me that he and Number Three had separated. He then booked us into that hotel, and we lived there for about six months. I then turned seventeen. I was so embarrassed. We moved to my father's stepfather's property and stayed there for around a month. My step grandfather tried to get into my bed with me. He scared me. He said he had made a mistake and had got confused. We moved out straight after then and lived with one of my father's friends for a couple of months. From there, we moved to another hotel and stayed for about six months. I had no stability at all during that time. I felt lost and lonely and I missed my brother a lot. Sometimes, I thought I could hear his music playing. Other times, I was sure I could smell his aftershave.' Tears were welling up in her blue eyes, and her voice was cracking.

'It's ok to cry, Sammy. You have gone to hell and back emotionally. You should cry, let your feelings out,' Dr. Hatton said quietly, and she saw that he too had tears in his eyes.

Sammy's whole body shook, and she began to sob. She had been taught not to cry and to get on with it by her father. To him, crying was a weakness. It felt good to be given permission to cry. She thought that once she started, she may never stop. Through the tears, she said quietly, 'My father will never let me have any time off.'

'Can you go on with your story? Can you tell me why you are referring to your stepmothers by numbers?' Dr. Hatton looked disgusted.

She thought about it for a second and responded, 'He told me to.'

'Go on, tell me more,' Dr. Hatton probed deeper into her childhood.

'The next year, my father bought a house. I had by then moved jobs to work at a different hotel. I had no idea of my father's personal life at the time. He rarely spoke to me, but I remember him telling me, "It's just us now, Sammy." I was relieved to finally have a place to call home and my own bedroom. However, shortly after we moved in, Number Three and her kids moved in. It was very confusing for me. I joined his company full-time then, and Number Three and I worked together. My father's relationship with her effectively ended in or around December. They were in their bedroom one night when she started screaming. My room was on one side of their bedroom; Justin's was on the other side. Justin and I had both heard the commotion and came out of our respective rooms to see her standing there with a nosebleed. Justin then punched my father. I instinctively hit Justin back. There was a scuffle at the top of the staircase. I left the house ten minutes later, furious, and went to sleep that night at the hotel where I worked.' Sammy's head hung low as she felt as if a huge weight was pinning her down. She barely continued, 'A removal van came to our house a couple of days later. She came with her parents, collected her belongings, and left. I never saw her again. My father and I visited his solicitor. I recall that my father signed documentation removing her as a shareholder. I watched him forge her signature.'

Dr. Hatton shook his head. 'Good grief, I think I need to see your father too and your biological mother. Would they be willing to come for family counselling?'

'I will try my best.' She paused and asked hesitantly, 'So do you think I am being haunted by my brother?'

'No, Sammy, you are grieving and you are very unwell. You will be fine with the right care. You really need to get together with your biological parents and talk things out. Ask them both to contact me, would you? Your session is up now. I will see you next week, same time and day.'

'Thank you, Dr. Hatton.' She smiled and a tiny bit of hope entered her heart. Maybe, just maybe, she could sort her feelings out. She needed six months off and complete rest. The thought sounded idyllic. Obtaining it would not be an easy task. She knew her parents would not take this news well.

The late afternoon sun was setting and it was chilly. The autumn leaves were turning. She loved this time of year. The colours were golden, red, and orange, just beautiful. She turned the radio on and out sang Donna Lewis. 'Feels like I'm standing in a timeless dream of light mists, of pale amber rose.'

Sammy began to sing along. Therapy felt like a different planet. Someone was actually interested in how she felt, she had time to talk, and she felt heard for the first time.

She called the office. 'Hi Becky. Listen, I won't be back in this week. I have tonsillitis. Ask William to call me at home when he rings in, would you, please?' she asked.

'OK, no problem. He has called already today, and he doesn't sound too impressed that you are not here,' Becky sounded worried.

'Thanks for the warning.' A frown appeared on her forehead as she hung up. When was he back from Phuket? Seemed like he was always on holiday these day with the new squeeze. What was she now? Twenty years his junior? She had acquired the salubrious title of 'Number Five'. It made her want to vomit. Dirty old man.

She decided just to go with the tonsillitis story until he came back the following week. She couldn't tell him about what the doctor had diagnosed or prescribed over the phone. She didn't relish the thought of telling him to his face either.

'Just put it to the back of your mind and face it when he comes back,' she told herself. 'If the doctor says I have to take time off, he will have to listen. It's not like I am skiving off.'

The counselling session that morning had opened her up, and she couldn't now stop the outpouring of her feelings about her past that she had driven to the far back of her mind. Like an earthquake, she found herself erupting and telling the Dr. about Number Four, or Four, as she referred to her.

'I was introduced to the woman who became my father's fourth wife the week of my eighteenth birthday. She had two children eight years and ten years my junior. I had not previously met any of them. I found they had moved into our house one evening after returning from London. It was a complete and utter shock as Number Three and her children had not been gone long, probably a couple of weeks. I was really upset. My father told me Four was in some sort of trouble and needed a place to stay for a while. As usual, I didn't get the opportunity to voice my concerns or how I felt. I was expected to comply and I did. Thank god I was driving. I went out most of the time. I felt invaded.' Sammy sighed heavily.

'Number Four? What do you mean? He has been married four times?' The Dr. looked shocked.

'Yes, four times so far. I did not get on at all with Four. In the beginning, I tried to make friends with her. I took her and her kids out, but no matter how hard I tried, she was not at all nice to me. She began to rearrange the house to her liking, which included moving all of my personal belongings from around the house and into my room—things such as books, shampoo, toiletries, and photographs. She then began to ostracise me from the dinner table. She would cook dinner for her, the kids, and my father and not include me, and he never said anything. He just let her do it. I was horrified.' Sammy felt angry now, really angry. She hadn't really realised how angry she actually was, and she felt livid as she relived it. 'In the months that Number Three had not been there, I had done all the household chores, including cooking, washing, and shopping. Four completely took over. It was as though I didn't exist. She would remove my washing from the washing basket and throw it back in my room. She then started to be really vile and threatened me with getting me out. She would say, "I will soon get you out of here. This is my home now—your father hates you and wishes you were dead, not your brother."

'When my father was out, she would also shout through her bedroom wall, which was next to mine, "Your father was incestuous with you and your brother, you are no longer of use to him. You will soon be out!" Sammy's anger turned to hurt and the tears welled up again. She felt embarrassed and turned away stuffing her feelings back down. 'I can't even bring myself to say her name,' she whispered.

'He allowed it to continue, and his attitude towards me was hostile. When he was going away for two weeks abroad with them, I was not invited and I was told to feed the dog. He left me a fiver and told me not to tell her he had given it to me. I was totally depressed and felt I was losing everything. I turned to Number Two for emotional support, but she was drunk and distant. She had been drunk constantly since my brothers' suicide. On their return from holiday, Four launched into me about various things that I was supposed to have done, from not feeding the dog properly and leaving the house a mess. I lost it and shouted back at her, "Fuck off!" I was totally distraught and could not stand this woman any longer. I could not understand why my father had taken her and her family in and completely shunned me. He sided with her and then told me to get out and threw my cases at me. "Change your attitude and don't come back till you do, Sammy." He locked himself in the bathroom and ran a bath. Four went and grabbed a load of black bags and started throwing my belongings in them, taunting me and saying "Don't forget anything."' Sammy felt that she had gone too far. Why was she telling this complete stranger her deepest feelings?

'Where did you go then?' he enquired.

'I left and moved in with my stepsister, who had moved back to the area. She said I could live in her flat for a while.

'My stepsister was renting the flat. I stayed there for around three months. I did stay at the business, although my relationship with my father during this period was volatile. The other two flatmates were employed as civilian admin officers for the police. My relationship with my father was severely strained, and the reality was that any woman that came on the scene attempted to push me out of the picture. He didn't want me in his life whenever a new family came on the scene. My relationship with Number One was non-existent. Number Two was by now an alcoholic. I joined the Military Police in 1987 as I was dating a solider at the time and he told me what a good life I could have away from home. On joining, I found I loved it. I did find discipline and self-esteem. I was praised for the first time in my life. I discovered a world where I was not some troublesome stepchild but a real person who was respected and liked. Both my colleagues and instructors seemed so sensible and calm, helping to nurture and stabilize me. I decided that I wanted to make the police my family, somewhere I could feel safe and help others who had been abused, assaulted, and bullied.' She looked sad.

'I was offered a job by police in July 1989. My recruitment officer did say that they suspected I had emotional difficulties and told me they were concerned by the fact that I was "hard faced". I was completely honest with them, and they accepted that with the passage of time and being away from my father, I would be in a healthy environment and lose the rage! I had sought counselling from my doctor when I was eighteen as I would have quite violent mood swings which were affecting my relationship with my boyfriend. I knew I had to get away from him and his toxic environment, so I resigned. I did not inform my father that I had applied to the force, and my resignation came as a shock. His reaction was to threaten me with arrest if I did not immediately give back my company car. His reaction was typical, irrational, and consistent with his behavior. I didn't return the car. My father's threat never came to fruition.' She felt the all-too familiar rage return and noticed her fists were clenched.

'How old are you, Sammy?' asked Dr. Hatton.

'Twenty-seven going on ninety-two.' She couldn't help laughing. It felt good to talk.

Driving to her friend Karen's, she reminded herself of how lucky she was to be off work for a while. Karen answered the door with Chloe, the Labrador, in tow.

'Are you coming on your holidays, Chloe?' Sammy chirped.

After a couple of glasses of Châteauneuf-du-Pape, they exchanged goodbyes, and Chloe jumped in the car. Sammy would be dog-sitting for a week, and Chloe was gorgeous. Sammy was looking forward to it and her much-needed time off work. Her father was back the following week, and she could tell him what was happening then. Things had been really strained between them, but then again, they always had been. Chloe followed her to the house as Lionel shot off in a panic. Chloe lived with three cats, so she took no notice. Lionel, however, was not so accepting. It was comforting having a dog in the house, and they snuggled up together, listening to a meditation CD. Sammy lit her scented candles, dimmed the lights, and as she reflected on the day. She felt strange. It was as though her heart was being ripped to pieces, and she was totally overwhelmed. She was changing dramatically with every childhood memory that surfaced. Therapy was very much on her mind.

It was still lonely living on her own, and she wondered if she would ever have a decent relationship. All her friends were married and talking about children, and she was single. A clairvoyant had told her that year that she would be alone for many years; she had also warned her about the kind of company her father was keeping. She remembered the evening she had organized at his house with the girls. They had all had their reading done, and Sammy had quite a shock when the clairvoyant told her there was an evil spirit in the house that had it in for her. She knew instantly who it was. She remembered Four vividly.

The only time she had with her father from the day he excluded her from home to her last day working at the business was strained. They only met during office hours and spoke purely business. She did not visit his home or have any contact with Four. She simply got on with the job to the best of her ability, although she was angry most of the time. Her father never spoke about real life, emotions, joy, sadness, hate, or despair; he was like a robot, a business machine. If she attempted to broach any subjects such as her brother or being thrown out, then he would respond with, 'Shut up. Haven't you got work to do?' For the first months that she was in the police, contact with her father was again strained. She invited him to her passing-out parade, but he declined the invitation. She was upset by this as she wanted him to feel proud of her. She tried to repair the rift between them and went to his house. She really did not know what to expect, but she was invited in. She told him that she would like to maintain a relationship with him, and he agreed to meet for lunch that week. During the time she was a police officer, she used to meet him on a monthly basis for lunch.

They would meet away from his home. She could not go into the house because Four would make it too difficult for her and hurl abuse at her. She was tempted to lock her up for breach of the peace, but didn't want to mix her family life with work. No one at work really knew her past, and she wanted to keep it that way. There was one incident when she went to collect the rest of her belongings soon after she was thrown out and was greeted by Four's son. He shouted to his mother, 'That bitch is at the front door!' What a terrible outburst from an eleven-year-old! Sammy's heart just sank, and she gritted her teeth and got her things.

She made her own life from there on in. Life was better. She could forget the unstable years and try to make a peaceful life for herself. She excelled in her career and was put on to a rapid promotion scheme; she got a mortgage enabling her to have her own house and privacy. She read books, wrote poetry, and listened to music. For once, she felt the sun on her face and the wind in her hair. She was free of her father's erratic lifestyle, but her sadness never faded.

Six years passed as she climbed the career ladder and lived a relatively normal life. She went out with the girls at weekends, had a few laughs, she danced, and had lots of boyfriends, though nothing serious. Her heart had been broken at an early age by her brother and her father, and it was now locked away, her emotions detached, much to the annoyance of her spurned lovers. Getting married and having children was not on her list of wants or needs. As January blustered and blew the crisp white flurries of snow on the ground, she received a call. The phone call changed her life again and set her on a collision course with disaster.

'Sammy, it's the foreman. Your father's in the hospital. He's had a really bad heart attack. I think you better get down there. Oh and don't tell his wife I called you.'

'Why not? What's it got to do with her?' She was enraged and put the phone down, then quickly redialed her father's home number.

'Hello.'

She recognized Four's voice and felt the urge to scream at her, but she remained calm.

'What's happened to my father?'

'How dare you phone here, you spoilt little bitch? Who told you?' Four spat down the phone.

'None of your business. You can't go anyway. It's only next of kin that can visit, and that's not you, is it? He doesn't want to see you anyway.'

Sammy put the phone down, cutting off the vile words and called her stepmother.

'Seven-seven-two-six, Hellooo?' Her stepmother sounded drunk.

'Mom, Dad's had a heart attack, and I can't go and see him according to that horrible woman!' Sammy's tone was desperate. As much as she was the professional police officer who could cope with the world's emergencies, she went to pieces dealing with her own.

'That's a lie, Sammy. Just call the hospital. They will tell you where he is and just go. Ignore her,' her stepmother suggested.

'Thanks, Mom. I will call you later.' She hung up, grabbed her coat, and drove to the hospital.

When she arrived at his room, he was alone. He was very upset and looked terrified. He told her he was scared and that he thought he might not live. Sammy fought hard not to look too upset but found it extremely upsetting. She took him a card and some extra-strong mints which she knew he loved. He told her that she could only stay a while as Four was due to come, and she would not be pleased to see her there.

She left dismayed. 'Why did he bow down to that horrible nasty woman? What the hell was wrong with him?' Sammy was his daughter, not his enemy. She subsequently visited him every day for a fortnight, noticing on the second visit that the card was gone and so were the mints. He had told her what time to visit each day so she would not cross paths with his wife. It was ridiculous.

Once he was released from the hospital, he went straight back to work against the advice of his doctors. His attitude was 'Who else is going to run the company?' They continued their lunches, but it was weekly rather than monthly. It was during those lunches that he began to plead with Sammy to resign from the police and return to the company. Her father was frail and seemed to have aged. He had lost weight and seemed extremely anxious. The sparkle had left his eyes. She recalled him bluntly asking her to return as a matter of urgency. It was more like an order than a request. When she called into the company on a daily basis, the foreman would frequently put pressure on her. 'You should be here with your father. He is not well. You are his only family.'

Every time she saw her father, he asked her if she had decided yet whether to return. He said she would return as the commercial director as it seemed to him that she had grown up and matured during her army and police service. He would entice her, telling her how they could become close again and create a dynasty.

'You will be a millionaire. The world will be your oyster. Who else do you know your age who can have all of this?' he boasted. He formally introduced her to key members of staff. 'This is Sammy. She will be taking over the company. I am going to groom her for success, and she will take the company into the twenty-first century.'

It was obvious from their discussions that he was concerned as to the future of the company and ensuring that the driving force behind it was someone from his bloodline. He told her that he wanted her to carry it on and then for her future children to do so afterwards. Sammy's view was that he believed at the time that he was not going to recover from his heart attack. She also knew that his marriage with Four was failing. He told her that they had been fighting and that she was psychotic. He also told her she was so nasty to her children that they would wet themselves. In their latest row, she had scratched his Lotus with her keys and thrown a brick through his window at the office. It followed that Sammy knew that if her father did not properly recover from his heart attack and died, there would be nobody in his life to whom he wanted to leave his estate. But what about Sammy? What did Sammy want? He didn't care. Her fate was sealed.

CHAPTER THREE

Reflection

Chloe snored. It was terribly funny to hear. Lionel had curiously come back, and they had made friends overnight.

She began to write, not too sure where to start, not sure whether she could face it. She was still haunted by her brothers' suicide and still very angry with her parents. She had opened up to Dr. Hatton about the suicide; she had yet to tell him about the next one. As she wrote, she was taken back to the midsummer of 1993.

Sammy and her father shared an office for the first few months after her return. Sammy saw it as her responsibility to ensure that he was able to relax and get better. She took most of his telephone calls so that any stress would be kept to a minimum. He did not mention too much about Four but Sammy got the impression that she was none too impressed by her return. She made a lot of telephone calls to the office which Sammy answered. Four would be hostile. 'Can I speak to my husband?' she would snarl. Sammy found this to be rude and childish. She never said 'Hello' or 'Can I speak to your dad, please?'

Working in the police was a very sociable job, and colleagues on Sammy's old shift were always going out to social functions. She maintained contact with them this way, and former colleagues would often call in for a quick cup of tea as the company was on her former policing division. One morning in early October, her father was late for work. This was very unusual as he was a stickler for time and could not abide lateness. Mobile telephones were not in popular circulation at the time, and nobody had a clue where he was. He arrived at approximately 10.30 a.m. and looked like he had seen a ghost. Sammy could tell by his face that he was in shock. He was as white as a sheet and had a nervous look in his eye. 'What's the matter?' Sammy asked him, eyeing him with suspicion and concern.

He broke down, 'One of us had to go. It was me or her.'

Totally distraught and on the verge of a breakdown, he then continued to tell her that it was over between them and he had packed some of his belongings as he wasn't going back home. After discussing the matter with him further, he was adamant that he did not wish to return to his home. Sammy offered to accommodate him at her home, which he accepted, and they went to her house. Sammy realised it was the first time he had been to her home. He was disheveled in comparison to his usual immaculate self. He took a shower and Sammy ironed his shirt for him. He then insisted on returning to work. He spent a quiet time in the office, and Sammy instructed the receptionist to block all their calls. She booked him into a local hotel, and he went there after close of business. Sammy had joined him for dinner in the hotel restaurant and then spent the evening in the bar. Leaving at about 11 p.m., she returned home. The telephone answering machine was blinking and full of messages. Listening to the messages, Sammy began to realise just what had happened. Four had been found dead at her father's home that afternoon; she had gassed herself with carbon monoxide in her Mercedes on the drive. 'Oh no! Not again, not another one.' And then sudden shock at the outrageous thought that came into her head, 'He has killed her.'

Sammy made relevant enquiries with the police and ascertained what had happened. The police were already involved, the body had been moved, and the house secured. Four's former husband had been called and had taken his children away with him. By this hour, it was very late, and Sammy decided not to inform her father until the morning as she saw no point in waking him up as there was nothing he could do and it would be pointless to disturb his sleep. She decided to inform him in the morning.

She arrived at the hotel at 8 a.m. and could tell instantly by his face that he already knew. Again, that thought, her inner voice was screaming, 'He killed her. It wasn't suicide.'

Sammy went to the house to check on the situation; the Mercedes sports car that Four had allegedly committed suicide in was still in the drive. Sammy later removed the car to a local car dealer, ironically a friend of her father's. She felt violently sick as she drove the car; the scent of death was all around her. Four's suicide didn't seem to affect her father even though she took her life at his home and in the same manner as his son. The death was recorded as a suicide. She had left a suicide note explaining that she could no longer cope with the mental cruelty that he was inflicting on her. Sammy was not in the least surprised.

Sammy's fingers flew across the keyboard like they were possessed. The pages filled with words. She didn't recognize the story. It wasn't hers; it was someone else's. She had disassociated from it all and was writing in the third person. She was trance-like, thoughts and feelings spinning through her mind. It was as though a deep dark well had opened up in her and she had fallen head first into it.

She was unveiling a depth of feeling she had never experienced before. It felt more like free association than writing. It was dawning on her that her father would be back on Monday, and all hell was about to break loose. She became even more withdrawn and ignored the telephone ringing. She had lost interest in the outside world.

The telephone rang and she grimaced when she heard the message on the answer phone.

'Sammy, it's your father. Where are you? Why are you not at work? Call me immediately when you get this message. Are you ill?'

At 7 p.m., her father arrived. He looked tanned and relaxed, whereas she looked tired and pale. 'I heard you were ill. What's wrong then? When will you be back in the office? You know how busy we are.'

'I have seen the doctor and a psychologist. I am not well at all. I need complete rest for six months and long-term therapy. The therapist wants to see you and my biological mother too.'

His face went a kaleidoscope of colours, first white, then green, then blood red with fury. 'If you come at me, Sammy, I will come twice as hard back at you,' he spat the words at her and clenched his fists.

"You will come back to work immediately, young lady. I am god round here, and you will do as I say.'

Sammy fell silent. It was a worse response than she expected. Pulling herself together and using what little strength she had left in her, she stood up to him. 'I will not come back to work until I am well enough to do so. I have a note for three months.'

'You must be fucking joking. You are not taking three months off. I will come and see this so-called mind-bender and tell him exactly what you need. I am not paying you to sit on your arse all day doing nothing. This is an outrage! What the hell is wrong with you?!' He stood, hands on hips, in his suit, glaring at his daughter.

'Look around you, my girl, and see all that you have. I gave you it, and I can take it away just as quickly. You are nothing without me. You call that so-called doctor of yours and make an appointment. I will be delighted to put him in his place.' The door slammed behind him.

'Oh, this is just great,' she thought. 'What a nice peaceful weekend, just what I need when I am signed off with stress.' She sank into the couch with her head in her hands. 'I am trapped. There is no way he is going to comply with this. He will make my life hell on earth. Oh god, what am I going to do now?'

Big wet tears of despair ran down her cheeks as her body wracked in excruciating emotional pain.

Chapter Four

Slave Labour

The business was growing enormously and Sammy had a pivotal role. By contrast, he was taking more time off. She had worked her hardest in her new role and felt she had to work even harder to prove herself. She didn't want to be seen as 'the boss's daughter'. She had more to prove than anyone else, and she felt so young and inexperienced in business. The foreman, and a couple of disgruntled old employees from the factory had not accepted her return very well. The fact that she was a former police officer didn't go down well with some employees, who were nefarious characters from the local council estate. These people were cannon fodder, brainless, lifeless idiots that worked on machines all day and had been bought up to hate authority. She often smelt the whiff of cannabis from their canteen and heard the whispers behind her back. Fortunately, she had broad shoulders and ignored the gossip.

The initial few months were extremely busy as, unfortunately, two key female members of staff had walked out after an argument with her father. She was literally thrown in at the deep end and continued to develop the company on her own volition. She suggested to her father various methods to enhance the company as she had just left an employer who was far more advanced in terms of administration, business law, and procedures. She did not get involved in production at all. The company really was in turmoil when she re-joined, having lost its head of administration and the wages clerk. She hit the floor running and had little opportunity to discuss anything about progression for the first few months. She approached her role as a director with great energy. The relationship with her father began to improve. She began to travel abroad as her business acumen grew, and she was forging relationships with customers both in this country and overseas.

Her first major task was to recruit and restructure. She interviewed and employed a new receptionist and assigned and retrained existing employees to manage the purchase ledger and administration, giving them both additional responsibilities beyond their current remit. She recruited new sales representatives and new sales coordinators to work alongside them. She then interviewed the two existing sales representatives for the position of sales manager, having them psychometrically tested to ascertain the best candidate for the role. She considered, then brought to fruition, the restructuring and assignment of sales coordinators to sales representatives and assigned specific geographical areas of the United Kingdom and Ireland for each. Each sales representative had their own dedicated sales coordinator and a geographical area to sell in.

She discovered that being a commercial director had its drawbacks as well as obvious financial advantages; she was shattered most of the time. Negotiating with the existing landlords with a view to obtaining some more office space, she got the lease for the building next to the existing office on the same industrial estate. She designed the office space in the new building so that it would achieve maximum productivity and house new computers and office furniture, allocating the administration and sales departments into the new premises to encompass the restructuring and growth that she was endeavoring to oversee. She used the new premises to house the new staff and deal with the growth that the company was experiencing, leaving manufacturing and transport in the old building where her father's office was.

As part of her new responsibilities, she conversed and worked with a computer programming company with a view to installing a new computer system. This dealt with the keeping of customer records, and in addition, she introduced a computerized stock-taking programme, which enabled the company to calculate accurate costs, thus increasing profits. The old telephone system could not cope with the increase of business, so she also updated the system, enabling more calls to be taken and for direct lines for customers to come straight through to sales coordinators. This inevitably led to improved customer satisfaction and a greater ease for customers to order goods. Mobile telephones had just come on the market, so she also sourced and implemented mobile telephones for sales representatives and introduced customer call records for each visit. These, in turn, were inputted into the customer records so that staff knew the current position at any given time.

In October that year, she trained in ISO 9002 to enable the company both to acquire some uniformity and to enable it to conform to British standards. As a result, the company became suppliers for customers such as local councils, again increasing turnover. She would come home at the end of the day completely exhausted. The company seemed archaic in comparison to the police, with its outdated thinking and lack of information technology, so she took it upon herself to change the company's policy of weekly cash payments to monthly BACS payments ensuring that time management was improved by all members of staff and that the personnel records of all employees were completed and accurate.

Sammy had always been one for improving her mind and was usually on a training course of some kind; she thought that this ethos would suit the employees, so she initiated an education scheme, whereby employees were encouraged to attend higher education relevant to their particular job specification to enable them to improve specific skills. For the sales staff, she negotiated and purchased company vehicles, introducing mileage and damage reports, keeping them roadworthy and ensuring accurate mileage for tax purposes. Her organization skills were enviable. As her confidence grew in her abilities, she organized and attended several exhibitions in the United Kingdom and Ireland, meeting and discussing with other directors the possibility of joint ventures. She began to travel as an ambassador of the company to Canada and Dublin to discuss and exchange examples of productive and profitable schemes of work. She would be away weeks at a time, and her social life was becoming non-existent. Her friends would call her often at work or home, but she rarely had time to return their calls.

Throughout her employment as commercial director at the company, she herself attended college, studying BTEC, business and finance. She implemented proven business techniques that she learnt. She also attended various seminars and training days at the Chamber of Commerce in relation to 'time management' and 'increased sales'. The larger workforce increased the company's productivity and therefore its growth. The business took off partly as a consequence of her return and her commitment to hard work and received a Price Waterhouse award for the company's growth in respect of turnover and employees.

In the summer of 1994. Sammy suggested a garden party at her father's home for the staff and various friends. She arranged the party which included a barbeque, a karaoke, and a band. All the staff were invited along with her former police colleagues, whom she had remained in touch with. The party was successful, and the environment at work was very pleasant. She had doubled the sales staff, and turnover had increased significantly.

Sammy's relationship with her father blossomed, and she felt like a hole in her heart had been filled again. She was part of a family once more. They had lunch or dinner once a week, and she was a regular visitor to his home. She interviewed a housekeeper, and she worked three times a week looking after her father's domestic needs. Her father seemed to recover, and the pressure of a bad marriage had left him. He tentatively began to date again. The parties became a frequent and successful event. Life was good.

Sammy and her father would also attend an annual lunch at Claridges in London. They would stay at the hotel and take in a show at a local theatre. They spoke frequently about her succession, especially at these lunches as they travelled together by train and had a lot of time to talk. During 1993 and 1994, her father dated several women. None of those relationships were particularly serious, and he used to joke that he always had a 'Wednesday night woman'. He would always be seeing more than one woman at a time, and Sammy met all three. She was concerned in particular that two of them were twenty years younger than her father. She did like one woman who was her father's age and a probation officer. Her father later told her that the relationship had finished when she caught him with someone else and slapped his face.

Sammy's disposable income increased significantly, much to the envy of her peers. She had an all-expenses paid car, health care, dental care, and an American Express card. Her father would poke fun at her regarding her home and referred to it as 'the garage with a window'. This was due to the fact that it was a very small, three-bedroom, semi-detached house that she had bought when she was a police officer. Her father suggested that she should move up the property ladder and into a residence more suited to a commercial director.

Since her father separated from Number Two, they had not spent a Christmas together. He would go on holiday, and she would visit various friends. When Sammy returned to the company, she too emulated her father and went on holidays. Christmas was a deeply depressing time for her. In fact, she hated it. Birthdays were also a difficult time. Her father had thrown her eighteenth birthday party at the local pub. Number One had thrown her a twenty-first birthday party at the Police Social Club. Neither her father nor Number One attended the other's party. She would spend Boxing Day at Number One's house up until she was about sixteen.

When Number Two's relationship ended with her father, she had kept in touch with her on a regular basis. She met her around once a week for dinner, and occasionally, she stayed over at her house. Sammy got along very well with Number Two's new partner and went on holiday to Puerto Banús, where they had a motor cruiser moored. They would have a great time together whilst on holiday, but Number Two's drinking concerned Sammy. It was usual for her to drink a bottle of brandy a day, and sometimes, she would be in a drunken stupor in the middle of the day.

Number Two did receive counselling for her alcoholism, but she was unable to control it properly, and even spells spent at clinics did not improve her condition. It became embarrassing on occasions. She would forget that she had invited Sammy for dinner and would be drunk and unprepared when she arrived. Sammy attempted to provide her with the best help available, which included Harley Street doctors. Unfortunately, her attempts were in vain, and Number Two continued to drink. In May 1994, Sammy again holidayed in Banús with them. They had a great time, and Sammy really had always considered Number Two to be her mother. Unfortunately, going on holiday caused jealousy on the part of Number One, with whom she was in touch with on an intermittent basis. Number One had always tried to manipulate Sammy as a child, but as Sammy grew up and grew wise to her control drama, she ignored her. This behavior did nothing to repair the enormous rift that had been between them all her life. She wished that Number One didn't exist and felt an annoyance at her very being. Seeing her was a chore, not a pleasure or something Sammy would have taken to doing if she had a choice.

On 29 September 1994, her father came into her office and told her that Number Two was seriously ill in hospital. She immediately went to see her and learnt that she had liver failure; she was conscious, but very ill, frail, and yellow in colour. They had a brief conversation, but as she was very heavily medicated, she fell unconscious. Sammy rang her former stepsister and they met at the hospital. They both stayed at the hospital for two days; Sammy's house was very nearby. The doctors told them that Number Two was being kept alive by machinery and that she was clinically dead. Number two's daughter, as her next of kin, was asked to make the decision to turn the machine off. Sammy stayed with her former stepsister whilst she turned the machine off and watched number two die. She was forty-eight years old.

The funeral took place a couple of weeks later. Sammy's father attended together with her former stepsister and Sammy. They all sat together at the service. It was the first time they had been together since her brothers' funeral. Her brothers' funeral was on Sammy's mind as the curtains closed on Number Two's coffin. Her heart ached as she fought back the tears and knew she had lost another friend. She couldn't face the wake and made her excuses, fighting for air as she quickly drove away.

She returned to work the next day as she was scheduled to attend a training course. She was single and living alone and did not have any support as far as grieving was concerned. Her former stepsister lived in London and her father would not talk about it. Sammy learnt later that Number Two had continued to be her father's mistress after their divorce and his marriage to Number Three and Four. Number One relished the news that Number Two was dead. She began to want to get close to Sammy, but she was unable to reciprocate. Number One's partner then also began to put pressure on her to try to get close to her. Sammy was offended by this and thought he should mind his own business. His children had not kept in touch with him for years, and Sammy felt like everyone was pulling at her to do the right thing by them. They were not considering her feelings at all. Sammy's resentment towards them began to surface in her.

Sammy felt like she had entered into a tug of war between her father and Number One for her affections. She was also missing Number Two immensely. She became very depressed after the death and could not help but think her father had been instrumental in it. By November, she had sunk into the depths of despair and began to indulge in drinking too much herself. She took unnecessary risks and engaged in risky promiscuity. Her relationships with the opposite sex were purely physical; she had no feelings for anyone but fulfilled a primal need. Men came and went. She had no interest really. Work became her life. She was becoming like her father in many ways, and she didn't like the person she was turning into. Her financial wealth was increasing, but her emotional well-being was dangerously deficient. She had had the life force sucked out of her.

CHAPTER FIVE

Number Five

'When are you back in therapy?' asked Karen as they sat in the kitchen.

'Thursday morning for the next three months. I was a bit pensive before, but it is helping to clarify my thoughts and feelings. I am getting a lot of flashbacks, though I don't like them. I can't work out whether I am dreaming, hallucinating, or going totally crazy. I thought my dead brother had got into bed with me the other night, and Lionel had shit everywhere, it scared me. The therapist wants to see my biological mother and my father too. Jesus, those two in the same room after twenty-five years! That will be fun, not!'

'Talk to the therapist about it, Sammy. That's what he is there for. Don't be scared. You will get through this." She said reassuringly.

Sammy continued writing. Locked down feelings were coming to the surface—despair, anger, hurt, the emotions she had shut out for so long. She had been outside of herself, emotionless and living a barren, soulless existence. The padlock was removed, and her raw emotion surged to the service. Twenty-five years of pain, disgust, sorrow, and disappointment raged beneath her skin.

Tuesday and Wednesday passed without incident. Sammy was thoughtful; she walked across the fields and did a lot of thinking about her future. On Thursday she drove to her appointment with her therapist.

'So tell me, Sammy. Have you heard from him since Monday?' Dr. Hatton asked.

'Not a word. He is off sulking somewhere, I guess,' she answered.

'Give me his number and Molly's. It is imperative that I speak to them. Don't worry, this will be hard for you, but you have to stay strong.' He noted down the telephone numbers and asked, 'Is your father married now?' Sammy pulled a face and winced as though she had been burnt with a hot iron. 'There are two women with him now. I don't know what's going on. I have been told to stay out of his life by them. They have got it for me. It's like a script that runs over and over.' Sammy gave a heavy sigh as she sunk further into the couch.

'So do you want to tell me about them?' Dr. Hatton relaxed into his chair as he pulled his clipboard on to his lap. 'In November 1995, my father told me he had been seeing a woman and that he would like me to meet her. I agreed to this and asked how he had met her. He told me that he had been introduced to her by another female friend of his who was in a surrogate mother group. He told me that 'Number Five', as he calls her, had recently been a surrogate mother and that she lived up north. When I met her, she told me that she had been a surrogate mother out of love. I was suspicious of her and challenged her on her motives. She then admitted that she had been paid ten grand by the couple. I also understand that she is a trained masseuse; she brought her equipment to my father's house.' A look of disgust crossed Sammy's face.

'How did you meet?' He had been jotting down notes as she was talking.

'She arranged to come to my home for a coffee. I took an immediate dislike to her. There was something about her demeanor and actions that I didn't trust. I was concerned that she was twenty years younger than my father, and I thought she was trying to take advantage of him. I noticed that she had no idea about her body language and her proximity to me; she was right in my face. She would stand too close to me for comfort and ask all sorts of questions that frankly I did not want to discuss.'

'Did you tell your father how you felt?' he quizzed. 'There would have been no point in that. He carried on seeing her, and she began to come into the office. She always seemed to be looking for something, and in my opinion, she was being very nosey. I didn't like her coming into my office and would lock it in my absence. I had important documents and my father's will in my desk,' Sammy continued. 'I had arranged to go skiing for Christmas with a friend. We were due to fly out the day after the office Christmas party. She attended the party and bought me a gift. She encouraged me to open it in front of the staff. To my horror, it was several packets of condoms, a sex manual, and chocolate body paint. I was really embarrassed,' Sammy shook her head as she continued on. 'She very quickly moved in with my father together with her son, who was about seventeen at the time. He showered her with gifts, diamonds, holidays, a car, and private registration number. I knew that she was in a lot of debt before she met my father and that he paid it all off for her. I was at my father's house, and all the debt demands were there. There was also a handwritten list of all the money she owed. I asked her what it was, and she told me that my father was going to pay all of her bills. They had not been together that long, and he was still recently widowed. I think she was using him for his money.' Sammy looked concerned.

'I joined my father one evening for dinner at a restaurant, where I was introduced to Number Five's best friend Jane. She was my age and also from up north. She was pregnant and told me during the meal that her partner had refused to marry her and had ended the relationship when he found out about the pregnancy. She told me that my father had generously offered to pay for an abortion and put her up at his home until she was better. I nearly vomited over her at the table.' Sammy's face turned red and her eyes turned cold

'I don't like them. They are playing games with him,' Dr. Hatton replied.

Sammy carried on, though her tone had changed and her eyes had narrowed. 'Jane also became part of my father's life. I would not be surprised if my father was in a relationship with both of them at the same time. They seem to come as a pair. He is renowned for his generosity, and the pair of them were soon being wined and dined. I don't like them and think they are taking advantage of an old widower. Jane is very flirty with him, which I find to be inappropriate. My father looks like the stereotypical dirty old man with two younger women on either arm. It makes me feel quite ill.' She looked like she was about to vomit.

'You don't approve of the type of women he goes for, do you, Sammy?' he hit the nail right on the head.

'No one does. My aunts, his friends, the staff are all on at me to do something about it. What am I supposed to do? The gossip is rife.' 'How did he respond to that?' 'He has ostracised me again from his personal life, but expects me to carry on at the company and watch him make a complete idiot of himself. All of his friends and family are concerned by the motives of both of them. No one else has the courage to tell him what they really think. I get to hear of all of their concerns and they expect me to do something. I do and then I get ostracized. I consider myself to be a reasonably good judge of character, and I don't consider their intentions to be genuine. My father is recently bereaved, and I am concerned about his well-being. I am concerned for my future, because I can see history potentially repeating itself. I know how my father is easily coerced into almost anything by the promise of sex. He is crude and inappropriate in the company of women, including members of staff and my female friends. I have concerns about his conduct at work and have pointed out to him the possibility of a sexual harassment claim being brought against him.' Sammy looked sickened. 'He is a dirty old man.'

'What happened after you voiced your concerns?' Dr. Hatton asked.

'My father's best friend came to see me at the office. He told me that he was very concerned about him. He also thinks that Number Five and Jane are coarse and overtly sexual in restaurants and the casino they all go to. His friend told me that he had joined my father and Number Five over dinner, and she told him how she was "going to put me in my place". She is taking large amounts of money from my father by way of cheques and cashing them in at his local snooker club. She is also using the family surname.'

'How does that make you feel?' Dr. Hatton leant forwards, his clipboard firmly in his hand.

Furious. I confronted her about her words and actions. She started crying. I told her that I knew she was a gold-digger and that I would watch her very closely. My father was there at the time. He was shocked, seeing me like that, and accused me of holding a "kangaroo court". After this altercation she packed her bags and left.' Sammy paused then continued, 'It wasn't long before she was back, and my father stopped speaking to me. His attitude towards me now is hostile, and I am excluded from his personal life and his home. In the past, I have looked after his home when he goes away, but now I am told to stay away as Jane will be house-sitting. I can see my father getting closer to them. I am being pushed away like I am worthless whilst he showers these women and their families with anything and everything they ask for. It is coming off the company bottom line. I am not impressed. How would he feel if I did the same to him with some strange blokes? I am sure he would have a fit!'

Dr. Hatton paraphrased what Sammy had said perfectly. 'So you feel like you are not being treated equally as a director then? You don't agree with company profits being squandered on sex workers while you sit hard at work and he flys off round the world with them.'

'That is exactly right. Why should I work my damned self to exhaustion whilst they do nothing but spread their legs? I am not prepared to tolerate it. I am the commercial director, for god's sake! This is my future he is jeopardizing for the sake of some whores!' She felt the rage boiling within her.

'How are things between you now?' He looked concerned.

'Dreadful! I am being accused of things I haven't done. I was accused of damaging his snooker room with a knife when the damage was actually caused by her son throwing a knife around. He was seen doing this by the decorators and the housekeeper. Then, Jane accused me of trespassing at my own father's house! I've got a bloody key to the door, for god's sake! She phoned me at home and asked if I had been up that weekend and then told me I was not welcome without an appointment.'

'So how did that make you feel?' Dr. Hatton skilfully asked, bringing the issue into immediacy.

'I am not happy!' Sammy began to dwell on the story she had just told him, 'I am going to kill her.' She smiled menacingly as the words left her lips.

'No, you are not, Sammy. You are going to deal with all of your father's wives one by one, rationally, and in a safe environment. You may feel like you want to kill. That's a normal feeling, but we both know you are too smart and too clever to act on your feelings. Feel them all you like, shout, scream, or hit something, but don't go near your father, work, or any family at the moment. You are volatile right now.' 'I am not going to lift a piece of paper for that bastard or his whores ever again. Who the hell does he think he is?'

'That's good, Sammy. You just stay off work and distract yourself with pleasant tasks, write some poetry, take walks, do the garden, give it time, listen to the birds sing. I am signing you off for six months, and I am going to ring your parents. Leave things to me. I will see you next week. Oh, and if you don't want to answer your phone, then don't.' Dr. Hatton gave her a reassuring smile and winked at her. He saw her to the door and waved her off, scratching his head as he turned back into the door.

CHAPTER SIX

Descent into Drugs

Friday was glorious. For early October, the weather was still good, though the leaves had all but fallen from the trees. Her stepsister arrived with a look of concern.

'You look stressed Sammy, are you on any medication, have you ever smoked cannabis?' She eyed her quizzically.

"Last time was when I was at school, and it made me sick.'

'I smoke it at weekends. Do you mind?' she asked sheepishly.

'Why not? Lots of people do. Just open the window first.' Sammy was not really impressed, but there again, she was a bit boring when it came to drugs. Most of her peers outside of the police were doing recreational drugs at weekends, but she had been a police officer since she was eighteen, and drugs were not acceptable to her. She smiled to herself and wondered if she thought she was a stiff. She opened a bottle of wine and watched her roll a joint.

'Shall we put some soul music on? You have got loads of CDs. There must be a couple of hundred here.' She walked over to the tower and selected one of her favorites. The music drifted out of the speakers as the sweet sickly scent of marijuana filled the room. Sammy watched the smoke come from her lips and settle in a haze across the lounge.

Sammy drank her glass of wine. 'How long have you been smoking that for?'

'Since I was twelve. It's less harmful than alcohol and cheaper. Do you want a toke?'

Sammy pondered for a moment and replied, 'Might as well. I am in enough shit now as it is.' Taking the neatly rolled joint from her hand, she took a long drag and inhaled the toxic chemical deep into her lungs. She felt dizzy and sick and then burst out laughing.

'Oh, dear,' laughed her stepsister, 'you need to laugh more, you know. You are so serious about everything.' She grinned at her and laid her head back into the chair.

Sammy felt strange, like everything had slowed down. She had a fit of giggles and thought how she had never envisioned this scene, never in a million years. Here she was getting stoned with her former stepsister. The more she pondered, the more hilarious it became. The joint was doing its job. 'I am sooo much trouble. I can't believe he has signed me off for six months. My father is going to have a coronary! Bollocks to it, bollocks to all of it! I am fucked off with all of them.' She started to sing along with the music 'Easy like a Sunday morning, I wanna be high, so high . . .'

Sammy began to wonder how long it would be before someone came to disturb her. They smoked all weekend. It seemed harmless enough.

Monday arrived. She heard next door's dogs barking as they went for their morning walk; she rolled over to check on the time. She realised that she hadn't eaten anything in days; she had lost her appetite for food.

She played cards on the PC, and she was finally getting the hang of it. She even managed to complete the game once or twice. At around 6 p.m., the doorbell rang. 'Oh no, are you expecting anyone?' she asked her stepsister.

'No,' she responded. 'I will go upstairs out of the way.' She winked at her and disappeared into the bedroom. She couldn't believe her eyes as Number Five peered at her from the glass panel in the front door.

'What do you want?' Sammy glared at her.

'Your father is very concerned about you. Can I come in? I won't be a minute.'

'You have ten seconds,' thought Sammy as she opened the door and led her to the hallway. She hated her. She was in Sammy's opinion a tart, a gold-digging slut, who epitomised all that Sammy hated and fought against. This woman would open her legs for money. She didn't work, sold babies, and had no morals. She didn't offer her a drink; she didn't invite her to sit down.

'Why are you here? If he is so concerned, where is he?' She glared at her, disgusted at her and her father.

'He wanted me to come to see if you were OK. He wants to know when you are coming back to work. Is there someone here with you?' She looked behind Sammy and into the lounge.

'You cheeky bitch!' thought Sammy. She was doing his dirty work and trying to spy on her. Knowing the games well, she responded icily, 'I have submitted my doctor's note. I will be back when he signs me fit. Give my regards to my father and tell him if he wants to know how I am, he knows where I live. I will speak to the organ grinder, not the monkey. You know where the door is.'

Number Five turned on her heel as Sammy escorted her off her property. Sammy slammed the door behind her and went upstairs.

'Did you hear that?' Sammy was stunned.

'Cheeky bitch! I don't know how you didn't slap her.'

'I felt like it. I need a joint.' She wanted to feel nothing; she wanted to slow it all down. She attempted to roll her own to the delight of her stepsister, who laughed as she got it completely wrong.

'Here, let me teach you how.'
They spent the evening getting high and watching films. She knew a storm was brewing and was enraged at Number Five coming to her house. Of all the people she didn't want to see, Number Five had to be top of the list. She knew that something had to give between her and her father, but she was livid with him for the here and now and the past. She had had enough, and the thought of resigning had crossed her mind. She had studied employment law that year at college and knew he couldn't dismiss her whilst she was off sick. She breathed a sigh of relief as she took a sharp intake of the joint putting it to her lips, she thought, 'Fuck it, fuck everything!' The drug crept through her body, and she relaxed, smiled, and grinned as her mind closed.

Sammy began to shake, and complete terror took over her. She then thought about Number Two and had the overwhelming feeling that her brother and Number Two were about to walk up the path together.

In that moment, something took over her completely, an evil rage that overshadowed her every move. She was homicidal, she was suicidal; she started to scream. Rooted to the stair, she felt like the whole house was full of spirits, evil spirits. She could see nothing, but she felt them. Her mind filled with thoughts of Four. She felt the hairs on the back of her neck stand up and her senses heighten. There were others in the house with her. She was not alone. Blackness descended on the hall and on her. She was terrified and on her own as the ghosts of her past came to haunt her.

Sammy plunged head first into a dark pit, and the shit of her life pilled itself on top of her.

CHAPTER SEVEN

Doom and Gloom

Oxleys Hall became dark. The November winds howled through the courtyard as the snow began to fall. There were no lights on in her house, the light in her eyes had gone, and she was ghostly pale. She hadn't eaten. Food became a memory. All the joy had gone from her. Her hair hung limp. She no longer styled it. No make-up adorned her face. Her clothes hung loose. The rapid weight loss was noticeable, and it was dangerous. She looked ethereal. She continued to write on her laptop. She didn't recognise the words that appeared on the page.

She took a paintbrush from the garage and dipped it in white paint. She watched as her hand painted the hall wall in big white letters: 'William Davis is a bastard!' She felt like someone had taken over her. She felt possessed. She could sense that she was being taken over by someone else's spirit. The spirit was evil.

She became obsessed by thoughts of her brothers' and Four's suicides and began to plan her own. It was the only way out of her imprisoned life. She didn't want to live any more. She wanted to die. She hid herself away from the outside world and listened to her music. She began to write poetry and songs. The lyrics were dark and haunted—a representation of how she really felt. The mask she wore for the outside world was put away as her emotions came to the fore. The telephone began to ring. She heard it but it didn't seem real. She didn't feel in the same room as it, but she was.

'Hello.'

'Hello, Sammy. It's Dr Hatton. How are you?'

'Not good, really,' she replied. As the words left her lips, she felt a rush of emotion. It was like the dam holding in her tears had broken as she felt the surge of tears and the choking energy rush in her throat.

'I have spoken to your father and your mother. They are coming to see me today. I will let them know how we are progressing, and hopefully, by the time you come in on Thursday, I would have a schedule arranged for family therapy.'

'OK,' she whispered. 'Good luck. See you Thursday.' Her body keeled over into the foetal position as she sobbed. The pain was exhausting. She remained in the foetal position for hours. Lionel lay beside her on the floor under the desk.

She heard two car doors shut and to her disappointment saw her biological mother and her partner.

'Sammy, what on earth is a matter? You look awful. I haven't seen you for months. Where have you been? Her biological mother asked.

'You have upset your mother, Sammy. How could you do this to her? She has been upset by this therapy lark,' her biological mother's partner added.

Sammy looked at the two of them with utter disgust; she spoke the truth for the first time in her life to them. 'I have upset her! What about me? Have you ever thought how I might feel, you selfish prick? She left me, remember, to be with you! Or have you conveniently forgot? What does she expect?'

'How dare you talk to me like that? Look at your mother. You have upset her now.'

Her biological mother was holding her mouth and crying.

'Good. I am glad she is upset. Join the club. Who the fuck do you think you are? You are the fucking reason she left in the first place, you wanker! Get out of my house and stay out, the pair of you!' Sammy was livid. Her fists clenched as she squared up to him. She hated him with a passion and she let it show. 'Go on, fuck off!' she screamed. 'Get out!'

'Oh my god,' said her biological mother. 'What's happened to my beautiful daughter? That is not my daughter.'

'Your daughter? I am not your daughter. You are not my mother. You never have been. Chrissie is my mom and she is dead. My mother is dead, and you think you can take her place? After twenty-six years, you think you can hold my hand and wash my hair and take over? I hardly know you. You are some distant relation to me. I don't see you as my mother. I never have!'

'How dare you talk to your mother like that?' Her partner's face was furious.

'What the fuck has it got to do with you?! You are the bloke she fucked off with, remember? You can go and fuck yourself! Get out! Go on, get the fuck out, both of you!' Sammy moved closer to them, forcing them backwards and towards the door. She flung the front door open. 'Get the fuck out!' She then smiled a huge grin, then there was laughter and release. She had been dying to say that for years. 'Good riddance,' she thought to herself. Lionel was staring at her, his beautiful green eyes shining. 'Come on,' she said, 'let's go for a walk.'

She was shocked at her own behavior, but thinking about it as she walked over the field with Lionel, what she had said was the truth. She really didn't care for her biological mother and disliked her partner immensely. She had played a role in their lives that she neither enjoyed nor wanted. She had finally broken the chain. In Dr. Hatton's office, she recalled the previous encounter.

'It came out of me like an eruption. I knew I had felt like that for years. I didn't think I would ever have said it, though. Oh my god.' She looked surprised.

Dr. Hatton smiled and his reply was a comfort, 'You owe them nothing, Sammy, nothing at all. You have freed yourself from their guilt complexes. Did she always try to control you with guilt? Did she always try to steal your energy with her own control drama? She was playing "Poor Me". You should recognise it in the book I gave you to read.'

'Yes, I did. It really made sense to me, after all these years. I always felt really uncomfortable in their company, like I had to make up for something, like I had to make up for my brothers' suicide. They always told me I was all they had left. Jesus, what a weight on my shoulders that was! They made the decision to leave their children. What do they expect?'

'I spoke with your biological mother. She told me you have an older half-sister. Have you ever met her?'

'Once, years ago. She left her too when she was eighteen months old. She left her with her father. When I asked her about it, she reckoned that he used to beat her up. That's why she left. Who the hell leaves an eighteen-month-old baby girl with an abusive man? I think she is lying.'

'Oh yes, people can lie to themselves to justify their actions. Self-deceit is much easier than the truth.'

'You are right. What a bitch! Well, I think she knows how I feel about it now.' Sammy laughed and felt enormously relieved.

'My job is to help you self-actualise and help you to get rid of the control dramas people use to control you. You have some very strong characters around you, all competing for your love, time, and energy, and it has taken a terrible toll on your very soul. You are exhausted by it all. You have a hard trial in front of you, Sammy. Your father will be angry with you, but you have to stand your ground, no matter how hard it may seem.'

'He has threatened me already. He has threatened to withhold my wages. He can't do that. It's against the law. He seems furious.'

'I saw him on Tuesday. He is an assertive character. He is also delusional and has a narcissistic personality disorder.'

'I thought so. I thought he had changed over the years. He seems to get worse. He is an embarrassment. He totally embarrasses me in front of the staff and my friends. He chats my mates up. It's disgusting.' Sammy's face hardened.

'You don't like him, do you?'

'No, I don't, but I can't help but love him at the same time. It's confusing.'

'The father-daughter relationship is a complex one. Yours is incredibly hard due to the sheer number of women he has had in his life.

'I have just got on with it, but this time, I can't pretend to like his women. I think they are sex workers, and I am not prepared to lie. I can't be a hypocrite.'

'Then tell him. If he can't accept the truth, then he is being very immature. He should respect you as an individual and a woman.'

'That's the problem. To him, I am still fifteen. He can't accept me as a grown independent woman. He wants to keep me as a child, and I can't stand it. I wish I had never left the police. I hate working for him. I wake up crying sometimes and I am so stressed. His expectations are so high. I can't possibly live up to them.'

'What is the most important thing to your father, in your opinion?' he quizzed her.

'Money and sex,' she sighed. 'He is obsessed by both.'

'How does he control people?' He smiled wryly.

'With money,' she answered flatly. She felt so used.

'So give up the money and take control of your life. You had a decent job and salary without him. Go back to that, empower yourself.'

'I can't go back in the police. You can't just leave and return. It's against protocol. I am royally screwed now.'

'What do you want to do? You, Sammy?'

'I want to study psychology. Oh, and I have really started to enjoy writing. I have started to write poetry.'

'Excellent, you are nurturing yourself. Keep it up. You have to tell him that you are not going back to work for him. It will be the death of you.' He looked very seriously at her.

'That's easier said than done. He will go crazy. I am supposed to succeed him.' Her head hung low as she felt the tears welling up.

'That's his problem. You have your own path to walk. It's a very selfish person who enforces their will on another, very selfish indeed.'

'OK, I will tell him, but I want to do it here in your office with you some I feel supported.'

'Fine, I will ring him and get him to meet us here next Thursday. Is that all right?'

'Yes, fine.'

'Keep reading your book, Sammy. You will find life is about to change for you. If you can see the other person's control drama and bring it into the open, it loses all its power. Your father is a manipulator. You know that, and when he is not manipulating, he is interrogating. You are a sensible grown woman. You need to put an end to it and live your own life.'

'You are right. Thank you.' Sammy

Driving home she felt like she was floating on her return she ran a bath and picked up her book. She became engrossed as she read about control dramas. It was becoming clear to her just exactly how much she was being manipulated by others.

The week passed without incident. She read, listened to music, and wrote poetry. She began to think about Christmas and remembered she had invited her father and Number Five for Christmas dinner. She was regretting it.

On a bright snowy November morning, she drove to Dr. Hatton's house. She saw the Aston Martin parked on the drive. She watched her father get out; he was as usual immaculately dressed.

'Good morning, Sammy. You look pale. Are you eating? Do something about your spots while you are at it too.'

'Hello,' she said. As she looked at him, she realised they had no real bond, no real relationship. It was a farce, something put on for others to see.

Dr. Hatton opened the conversation, 'Sammy has something to tell you.'

'Oh no,' she thought, 'this is it. Just get it out of your mouth.'

'I want to leave the company.' She stared at him.

'You what?' Her father's face was like thunder. 'What did you say?'

'I am taking a career break. I want to go to university to study. I have finished my undergraduate course at college. The next step is university.' She continued to stare at him.

'Are you completely crazy? You are not going anywhere, my girl. You will come back to work as soon as possible. You have been off long enough. I want you back in the office on Monday,' he bellowed like a bull.

Sammy looked at the doctor.

'William, Sammy is in no fit state to return to the office. She needs therapy and she will not be returning to the office for some time. You need to accept what she has said.'

'Have you any idea what you are saying? Did you put her up to this? Have you twisted her mind completely? She is coming back to work whether she likes it or not.'

Sammy cringed in her chair. 'I am here, you know!' she said. 'I am not coming back to work. I am going to take a career break and study. It will be good for the company and help with human resources in the future.'

'What? What the hell do you mean? You are needed in the office. You have a role to fulfil. You're the commercial director, for god's sake. You can't just leave.' He looked like he was going to hit her.

'Sammy needs your reassurance that you will continue to support her financially whilst she takes time out. She needs to be able to pay her mortgage. Are you willing to do that for her?'

'I suppose so. Just how long will this be for?' His eyes narrowed.

'Five years,' Sammy replied.

'Sammy, it time for you to go now. I wish to speak with your father alone. I will see you next week.' Dr. Hatton put his hand on her shoulder and walked her to the door.

Sammy couldn't believe what had just happened; she was shocked, amazed, and delighted all at the same time.

'This can't be happening,' she thought. 'He has never just accepted that, has he? He is stalling. He will change his mind. He is just paying lip service to the doctor. I know him better than that.'

She couldn't help but doubt him, but as the cold wind blew through the bare trees, she felt a sense of freedom. Walking into the kitchen, she remembered what Dr. Hatton had said. Freedom could be obtainable; she had to give up the money at her disposal as a director. That was easy; she wasn't controlled by money at all. She was capable of maintaining herself. She reached into her bag, pulled out her purse, removed her company credit card, and cut it in half.

CHAPTER EIGHT

Cold December

December was freezing. Oxleys Hall was a big house to heat, and Sammy shivered as the snow piled up outside. She had disassociated from the company, her father, and Number One. She felt strange; it was as though a huge weight was lifted. She got herself organised and enrolled on her psychology course. She was due to start in early January.

She became almost reclusive and revelled in her new found distractions. She read and she wrote poetry. All the poetry was about how she felt about life. Her biological parents and the step-parents along the way had dished enough rejection between them towards her that it was no wonder she had an attachment disorder.

She attended her weekly session with Dr. Hatton. She was growing, and his expert knowledge was giving her the strength to continue.

'I want to hypnotise you, Sammy. It will help you to see this through. There is nothing to be scared of. You just need to relax.' He smiled reassuringly.

'Right, erm, I am a bit nervous really. When do you want to do it?' Her eyes widened.

'Now is a good a time as any. Don't look so worried. I wouldn't hurt you. Now go and lie on the couch. I am going to put a heart rate monitor on your finger, and then I want you to imagine you are on a beach and count backwards from one hundred.'

She lay down, her heart racing as she held her finger out to him. Closing her eyes, she began to count, 'One hundred, ninety-nine, ninety-eight, ninety-seven, ninety-six.'

She was completely under for the whole of the session. When she came back to reality, she couldn't remember a thing, but she felt serene. She felt angelic and she was peaceful.

'What did you do?' she questioned.

'I just gave you some positive self-image statements to help you through this, nothing more. Relax, don't worry. I will see you next week.'

Dr. Hatton smiled.

Sammy felt like she was floating. She put her car into gear and noticed that her fuel level was low. She drove to the petrol station where the company had an account. She filled up and went in to sign.

'Sorry, you are not authorised to use that account,' the cashier said.

'What?' A look of sheer disbelief came on her face.

'You can't sign any more, Sammy. Sorry.' The cashier looked embarrassed.

'On whose authority?' she enquired.

'William Davis.' The cashier looked awkward.

Sammy coul dn't believe it. What a pathetic, childish idiot! How petty could he get?

'Fine, I will pay cash.' She got the money from her purse and paid for the fuel.

She got back in her car and drove home. She had heard nothing from her father since their joint therapy session, nothing at all. This was his way of telling her he wasn't pleased; or as therapy had taught her, his way of trying to control her. She was ambivalent. She had savings, her own bank account, and she was still receiving her monthly wage. It had become a standoff; Sammy would not play his games and didn't call the office. She was now without her company credit card and a fuel account. The next shock came on payday. Her wages had been stopped.

In therapy, she told the doctor what had happened. 'I knew it. I just knew he would pull a stunt like this. He was bullshitting you. I told you he would punish me. I am signed off sick, for god's sake. He can't do this. I am going to have to phone him.' She was furious.

'Use my phone. Call him.' Dr. Hatton passed her the phone.

Becky answered the phone.

'Hi, it's Sammy. Can you put William on, please?'

Silence as the call was passed through and then.

'Yes, what do you want?'

'Where are my wages?'

She could hear the malice in his voice as he replied, 'I am god around here, Sammy. Did you really think I was going to pay you to sit on your arse? You stupid girl. You will get your wages when you come back to work.' He hung up.

Sammy was outraged. 'Oh my god, what am I going to do now? He is crazy. He can't do that. It's against employment law for a start. I am his daughter.' She was stunned.

'Do you realise now how he controls everyone in his life with money, Sammy? Have you ever considered why your brother, his friend, his fourth wife, and Number Two took their lives? How do you feel now? How are you energy levels?' Dr. Hatton looked at her.

'I feel awful, like I am totally drained, like my world is collapsing around my ears.' She began to sob as darkness and desperation surrounded her.

'You have choices here, Sammy. You will know what to do. Stay strong and remember everything will be OK.'

Sammy left the doctor and instinctively drove to an old neighbor's house. She pushed her mobile number through the door and drove home. Later that evening her neighbor called.

'Hi, stranger, long time no see. It's Andy. How are you?'

'Hi, did you take your employer to tribunal for constructive dismissal?' she asked.

'Yes, last year. Why?' he replied.

'I need your help. Can you come up, please?' she pleaded.

'Of course. I will be there in ten minutes.' He put the receiver down. Andy arrived ten minutes later and sat in silence as Sammy told him what had happened. He looked completely horrified. 'Jesus! What a bastard!' he said staring at her in disbelief.

'Tell me about it. He has given me no choice. What solicitors did you use?'

'Solomons in town. They are good, expensive, but good.'

'I will call them tomorrow morning.' Sammy sighed.

'You look terrible, Sammy.' Andy smiled.

'Thanks,' Sammy responded.

'Do you need some money?'

'No, Andy. I am OK for now, but thanks.'

Andy gave her a huge hug, and as he left, he turned to her and said, 'You know where I am if you need anything.'

Sammy smiled and closed the door. The huge weight had descended back on to her shoulders, and she shuddered from the cold air. 'I don't believe this is happening,' she thought.

She had lost nearly two stone in two months. Her clothes had begun to hang from her and her face was grey. She couldn't look in the mirror these days for too long. She looked haunted and gaunt. Sleep was impossible.

Her mind was reeling from the day's events. Her father's words rang in her ears. The image of him looking livid was constant. She felt like a startled deer trapped in the headlights. She wanted to run, but she was frozen. She wanted to escape, but where to? She had nowhere to go and no one to comfort her. She was alone, scared, and on the verge of becoming catatonic.

As she lay in her bed looking at the night sky, she began to question why so many people in her life had committed suicide. Was it to get away from that manipulative, controlling bastard? After all, he had been the common denominator for all of them. She knew the answer but didn't want to accept it. Horror gripped her as the suicidal ghosts from her past haunted her again. She felt the hairs on the back of her neck stand up, the tingle in her nose, and the now familiar feeling rise in her. She was not alone. Trance-like, she walked to her laptop and began to type, though it was not Sammy typing. It was the ghost of Four. 'M-U-R-D-E-R-E-R'

Sammy was terrified as her hands pressed the keys down.

'M-U-R-D-E-R-E-R'

She had to physically pull herself away from the desk. She wanted to scream, but no sound left her throat. She walked trance-like into the garage and stood staring at the hosepipe.

'Go on, do it.' Sammy recognized Four's voice in her head. 'Join us. It's the only way,' she beckoned.

Sammy tried to shut the voice out. She fought hard to run from the garage, but she couldn't. She was immobilised. Taking a paintbrush from the shelf, she dipped it into black paint and painted a huge inverted pentagram on the floor. It was not a conscious act. She had no control. Leaving the garage and the patio doors unlocked, she walked back upstairs and got back into bed. An unrecognizable male voice commanded, 'Get out of this house!'

Sammy was terrified and wondering what it was she was hearing, was it ghosts or was it schizophrenia? She crawled on to the floor and under the bed. Lionel walked into the room, his tail standing upright, his fur stood on end, his eyes wide.

'Lionel,' she whispered. Lionel jumped and hissed, then to Sammy's horror, defecated all over the bedroom floor. She opened her bedside cabinet, took a bottle of red nail varnish out, and scrawled on the wall.

'Help!' The brush and bottle fell to the floor and silence fell on Oxleys Hall.

She heard the key turn in the door as Tina, her cleaner, let herself in. 'Sammy? Are you here?'

'Upstairs.' Sammy sat motionless and terrified on the floor in her bedroom, the stale faeces all around her.

'Oh my god! What's happened? What's going on? Are you OK?'

Sammy stared transfixed at the writing on the wall as Tina coaxed her out of the room and downstairs. 'I am calling the doctor. Just drink this tea,

Sammy. I will clean up. Don't worry.' Tina's face was white. Her hands were shaking as she passed Sammy her drink and picked up the phone.

A general practitioner arrived. He fussed around Sammy with Tina, but she didn't hear his words. She was in shock. Sammy's senses were heightened, her mind totally focused on Four. Her demons had come back to haunt her.

'Is there anyone you can call to come and be with you?' enquired the GP.

'Nobody, nobody at all,' she replied.

'Here, take these. They are Lorazepam. You should sleep well. Take one anytime you feel anxious. I would normally recommend that you see a counsellor, but you are in private therapy now, so I suggest you keep seeing him and let him know what medication I have given you. Tina lives just down the road. She will keep an eye on you.'

She put the little blue pill in her mouth and swallowed. 'I am being haunted,' she said.

'That's not really my remit, Sammy. You should speak to your therapist about it. Get some rest, and Tina, call me if you need anything else.'

Tina saw the doctor out and said, 'Sammy, I have to go now. I don't know what to do for you. I am always here if you want to talk.' Tina looked sad.

'Tina, I am so sorry, but I can't afford to keep you on any longer,' Sammy said apologetically.

'I understand, but still you know where I am if you want to talk.' Tina smiled at her, though her face was etched with concern. 'Take care,' she said over her shoulder as she left the hall.

Sammy went upstairs. The drug was taking effect as she crawled into bed and pulled the quilt over her head.

Chapter Nine

Divine Intervention

In the morning, she drove like a waif possessed to her nearest church.

'Can I help you?' the vicar asked.

'I think I am being haunted. I think something is trying to harm me. I am really scared. Please help me!' Her eyes were staring and she looked really ill.

'Tell me what is troubling you. I am here to help.'

'I live in Oxleys Hall. There are strange things happening up there.

It's haunted. I can feel it. My cat has defecated everywhere, the lights have begun to flicker on and off, and I have heard footsteps and voices. I am terrified.'

'What do you think it could be?'

The question puzzled her, but she replied, 'I think it's my dead stepmother.

She committed suicide. So did my brother and my stepmother. I think they are having some kind of battle around me. I can't see anything, but I can feel it. I can't describe it properly, but I feel like I am caught in a big battle between good and evil. Sometimes, I feel completely terrified, and at other times, I feel so peaceful. I don't know what is happening Vicar, please help.'

'I will come this evening with my understudy. We will come to you. I think you are experiencing poltergeists. We will bless your house.'

'What?' Her face twisted in discomfort. 'How?'

'I will explain later when we get there. Go home and wait for us. You will be OK. They can't physically harm you.'

Sammy didn't want to go home. She couldn't call on anyone.

'She had become like an entity herself, not knowing who to cling to, not trusting her own mind, frightened and alone.

The vicar and his understudy arrived at 6 p.m.; they both looked concerned but not in the least scared. Sammy felt a sense of well-being and comfort as she let them in.

'What exactly has been happening?' asked the vicar as he sat down in the lounge.

Sammy knew she had to tell him everything from the start, all of the strange things she had encountered not only in the Hall but previously too.

'My brother committed suicide when I was fifteen. He gassed himself with carbon monoxide in his car in a country lane. Afterwards, sometimes at night, I could hear music playing from his bedroom, and I could smell his aftershave. Occasionally, when I was in bed at night, I used to get a really high-pitched sound in my ears and felt like my entire body had shrunk, like the bed had engulfed me. I would try to open my eyes to make it go away. I couldn't work out if I was dreaming or awake. I knew if I could just get my eyes open, the noise and the feeling of being tiny would go away. It was like my eyes had been forced shut. I would fight my hardest to open them but I couldn't. As it happened, I felt like someone was pulling me out of bed by my feet, trying to pull me upwards. I would be frozen in terror.'

'Did this happen a lot?' asked the understudy.

'On and off for ten years or so. I used to wake up crying.'

'Have you spoken to anyone else about this?'

'I have been to a couple of clairvoyants in the past, and they both said that there was a young man standing at my shoulder and that he wanted to say sorry. I took it with a pinch of salt really.'

'What has been happening here in the Hall?'

'Someone got into bed with me and hugged me. I heard a voice telling me it was beautiful and that everything would be fine. I thought it was my brother, but I could have been dreaming. I feel like I am being watched all the time. Like there's something behind that wall, looking at me.' She pointed to the lounge wall.

'Anything else?' The vicar looked at her.

'Every time I go to the toilet or have a bath or shower, I think there is someone else in the room with me. I can't see anything, but I can feel it.

The lights keep blowing. I have heard footsteps and heard knocking at the front door, but when I answered it, there was no one there.'

'Has anyone else seen or heard anything?'

'Yes, my friend Paula told me she felt like someone had put their arm around her as she walked up the stairs. The gardener said he had seen a lady in white in the garden and a child playing in the courtyard. They disappeared into thin air when I tried to see them. My cat is acting very strangely and defecating everywhere. A neighbour told me his little girl said there was a lady sitting on her bed late at night when there was no one else in his house, and the guy across the courtyard said he was pinned down to his bed by the throat!' 'Hmm.' The understudy looked thoughtful.

'I have felt like someone is trying to possess me. I have been writing things that I don't recognise. I have painted on the walls and floor and I can't remember doing it.' Sammy hung her head and began to cry. The look in her eyes was one of terror.

'You are experiencing poltergeists, Sammy, lots of them. They are like children, and they like to play tricks on you to scare you. A poltergeist is a paranormal phenomenon which consists of events alluding to the manifestation of an imperceptible entity. Such manifestation typically includes inanimate objects being thrown, electrical interference, sentient noises such as impaired knocking, pounding, or banging, and on some occasions, physical attacks on those witnessing the events. Since no conclusive scientific explanation of the events exists up to this day, poltergeists have traditionally been described in folklore as troubled spirits or ghosts which haunt a particular person—hence the name. Such alleged poltergeist manifestations have been reported in many cultures and countries, and the earliest recorded cases date back to the first century.'

Sammy's mouth fell open and her jaw dropped. She could not believe what she was hearing. 'So why me? Why are they haunting me?'

'They're spirits with unfinished business. Ones that can't cross over to the next life. They're trapped here. Those who commit suicide normally can't cross over. Suicide is a sin,' he offered.

Sammy understood what the vicar had said; she asked the question that was troubling her the most, 'Is it possible that a spirit can possess someone?'

'Spirit possession is a paranormal or supernatural event allegedly where spirits, gods, demons, animals, or other discarnate entities take control of a human body, resulting in noticeable changes in health and behaviour. The term can also describe a similar action of taking residence in an inanimate object, possibly giving it animation. The concept of spiritual possession exists in many religions. Possession may be voluntary or involuntary and may be considered to have beneficial or detrimental effects. A constant feature of possession is involuntary, uncensored behaviour, and an extra-human, extra-social aspect to the individual's actions. He is dehumanised, bereft of normal powers of recognition and reaction, and his speech and movements are distant from the societal norm.'

'Oh my god, you have to help me!' Sammy looked terrified.

'We will, Sammy. Just sit there and we will bless the house and you.' They stood up and each took out a bottle of holy water.

'I command you in the name of God to leave this place. I command you in the name of God to leave this place.'

Sammy sat transfixed as she watched them; they went into every room, repeating the same words. She was fascinated and terrified at the same time. They returned to the lounge. The vicar gave her a reassuring smile. 'Things should settle down now. Should you have any more trouble, come straight to church.'

'I will see you out and thank you.' She shut the door and slid down the wall, putting her head in her hands.

A week passed. It was silent. The telephone didn't ring and no one called. She drugged herself with Lorazepam. She drifted along, not eating, getting weaker all the time.

It was two days before Christmas. No decorations were hanging up, there wasn't a tree, and there were no presents. She noticed how beautiful but empty the Hall looked. Tired and alone, she climbed the stairs.
Crossing the landing, she let out a scream as she felt a pain across her back as a force she had never felt before threw her backwards down the stairs.
She desperately tried to stop her fall, but she hit the bottom step with the full force of her right foot. The pain was excruciating as her hip, and ankle dislocated. She crawled to the telephone, each agonising movement

sending waves of pain through her thin body. Calling 999, she managed to say, 'Ambulance, I have fallen. Please help!'

The ambulance crew gave her gas and air and took her to hospital, where she was injected with painkillers and X-rayed. She had dislocated her hip. She was treated appallingly by the staff, left in a corridor for hours; there was no bed available on the ward, so she was put in a stock room barely big enough to house her. No one visited. She didn't want to see anyone. She was suicidal.

Another week passed, and she discharged herself against the advice of the doctors. Calling a taxi, she wondered what day it was. She wondered how Lionel was. She wondered where her parents were. As the taxi pulled into the drive, she saw instantly that something was wrong. Her company car had gone. She instinctively knew her father had taken it back.

CHAPTER TEN

Hell on Earth

She typed her resignation and packed quickly, her life bundled into a suitcase, a few photos of happier times, her passport, and the little money she had left in her savings account. She asked the neighbour to feed Lionel and put the house on the market, leaving a key with the agents. She posted her resignation on the way to the airport. Her hip was still painful, but she kept walking.

She flew to Florida, a place she had been to many times before. She knew it well; she liked the way of life and the laid-back atmosphere. When she arrived at U.S. Customs and was asked 'Business or pleasure?' she replied 'A bit of both.'

She had taken a fly drive. She had no definite plans. She just had to get out of the country and away from the stress. The hire car was a convertible. She felt free as she dropped the hood and drove out of the airport, heading south on the freeway.

After a couple of hours, she pulled into a motel and checked in for the night. She opened the bedside drawer and saw the Bible. She had never read a page in her life, but she felt compelled to start reading it. It made little sense to her distressed mind. She sat in bed, her mind racing as she tried to rationalise what had been happening around her. She was not herself. She had lost her identity.

The sun came up bright and early, and she took a swim in the pool. It was January but still warm. The water soothed her nerves as she swam several lengths, stretching her pale thin body. She didn't recognise the figure reflected in the mirror.

After paying her bill, she continued south, then travelled southwest to the Gulf Coast. Palm trees swayed in the light breeze and pelicans flew in the blue skies. She curiously spotted a sign for Treasure Island. She smiled to herself and headed for the beach. It was stunning; the Gulf water was azure blue and beckoned her. She pulled into a hotel on the beach and checked in for a week. She still had no specific plans, but knew she never wanted to return to her old life.

Once her things were unpacked, she grabbed a towel and a magazine and walked down to the beach. It was a glorious day. She stretched out on her stomach and began to read. Her attention drifted away from the magazine as she watched the beach come to life. Families sat by the water, jet skis and boats sailed by, seagulls circled above, and the sun warmed her body and soul.

Through the afternoon haze, she saw him approach her; he was tanned, very handsome, and spoke with an American accent, 'Pardon me, Miss, I live right next door in that house. Me and my buddies are having a barbeque later, and you look like you could use some company. Do you want to join us?'

As she looked closer, she looked into his eyes. They were green. 'Oh, thanks very much. I am on my own, so yeah OK, I would like that.' She smiled back.

She wanted to get to know the locals and to try and find some sort of job, maybe rent a property on the beach; this could be a good opportunity to get to know people and the area. She gathered her things and joined him.

'My name is Theodore.'

'Sammy,' she replied.

'That's a terrific accent, Sammy.'

'Call me Ted, for short. My family is Italian American. There will be girls and guys around your age joining us later, so tell me how come you are on your own?'

Sammy sat with him outside on his porch right on the beach, and he introduced her to his dog, Riggins, a Dalmatian puppy. Ted handed her a cold beer. Sammy had been to Florida on business and on holiday some eight times before and knew how friendly Americans were compared to the British. She felt no danger with Ted. It was a sunny afternoon, and there were hundreds of people about. She told him about work, not everything, just the basics; she didn't mention Oxleys Hall. That would have been too much information. Ted, in turn, told her that he had recently separated from his wife, was renting the beach house, and was a stockbroker. As they chatted, his friends began to arrive. They all seemed very friendly, and she was soon talking to them—women, children, and couples. She had relaxed and began to envision a new life. They told her it would be easy to get work and that the costs of apartments or beach houses were not too expensive. She listened intently as she noticed how often Ted was looking at her. People began to leave as the barbeque wound down. She exchanged goodbyes and felt pleased that she had met some nice people; she was also very attracted to Ted.

'You don't have to leave just yet. Stick around for a while, and we can go for a walk on the beach. It's so pretty in the moonlight, just like you.'

Sammy blushed. 'Thank you. You can walk me back to my hotel, if that's not too far!' She laughed, seeing as it was twenty yards away.

'Great, let me get Riggins' lead, and we can get going.'

They walked out on to the beach, walking half on the sand and half in the water. It was still warm, and the moonlight cast a beautiful white light over the ocean. Ted reached for her hand. She allowed him to hold it as they fell into step together with Riggins leading the way.

Ted spoke gently as they walked past her hotel, 'I miss my wife, Sammy. We have been to counselling, but she has left me. I don't think she is ever coming back. We had some terrible arguments over money and me working late. She had had enough. She said I wasn't giving her enough attention.'

Sammy listened to him, aware that everybody had problems of some kind or another, aware that happiness was out of reach for many people.

'The beach house is still a mess. I haven't tidied up for a while. Sorry, I have just been so busy.' He looked embarrassed.

'Your house is lovely. I would love to live on the beach. You are so lucky. I want to stay here and find work. I can't go back home now. There is nothing there for me anymore.'

'What, nothing? No man in your life? You gotta be kidding me! You are stunning, Sammy! You have the most beautiful blue eyes I have ever seen!'
He stopped and turned to face her, putting one hand on her back and the other at the back of her neck. He pulled her towards him and kissed her.
Their lips touched and their mouths locked together in a passionate kiss.
He pulled her closer as lust gripped them both. The kiss grew in intensity as she felt herself becoming more and more aroused.

'Oh god, you're beautiful, Sammy. I want you so much. Let's get back.'

As the door closed behind them in the beach house, he pulled her on top of him on the couch as he kissed her again, his tongue exploring her mouth, his hands caressing her. As the moonlight lit the room with soft shades of silver and white, they made love. She awoke with her head on his chest, still on the couch. The first thing she heard was the ocean lapping against the shore. It was beautiful. He stirred and cuddled up to her.

'Come here, Sammy.' He nuzzled into her neck. She sought out his lips, and they kissed, reawakening the previous night's passion. They made love again. 'Come and stay with me. You can get a job here, Sammy.'

'Are you serious?' She laughed.

'Sure, why not? I could use some company, and I am totally enamoured with you.'

Sammy was stunned. She was not used to such bluntness, but she liked the idea very much. Ted had made her feel wanted again. She needed that feeling to replace the overwhelming rejection she had felt. Ted took them for breakfast as she giggled over the impossible amount of ways the Americans cooked their eggs. She had an English muffin and coffee and sat gazing at this handsome stranger who had rapidly become her lover. She scolded herself briefly for succumbing on the first night, then scolded herself again for being so childish. She was a grown woman.

'I will stay in the hotel for the week. I can look for work, and if things work out, I will think about your offer,' she told Ted as he tucked into his eggs.

'That's great, but hey! I have a cousin in Miami. Do you fancy going for the weekend? He lives in Coconut Grove. We can stay with him. His name is Mickey.'

'Great, I love Miami!' She had been there several times and loved it.

They spent the rest of the day on the beach, playing with Riggins and with Ted's basketball. They swam, hired a jet ski, and danced the night away at the bar. Ted had roller skates, and she put them on in her inebriated state and played pool. She felt fantastic, free, and full of life.

On Friday morning, she packed a few things, and they drove the four-hour drive to Miami. They laughed and joked most of the way. He drove as she took in the scenery. The journey passed quickly, and they soon arrived in Coconut Grove. She was stunned; it was salubrious, lush green palm trees, spotless streets, and beautiful buildings. Ted introduced her to Mickey, who worked for a local television company. They met up later with friends of Mickey's, an English couple who she hit it off with straight away, Simon and Claire.

The five of them went out for a meal and drinks and then danced till dawn in a club. Ted was chivalrous and attentive as she basked in his adoration.

'You are my English rose, Sammy. I adore you. Stay with me. Don't go back to England, please,' he whispered.

'I won't,' she replied.

She exchanged numbers with Simon and Claire, and they left the following morning, refreshed and excited about their plans. She checked out of the hotel and into his beach house. She did the spring cleaning for him as he worked from home on his laptop. Riggins followed her around the house and barked and pranced, pushing his ball at her to play. She was so distracted that all thoughts of her father, biological mother, and Oxleys Hall vanished. On top of her case lay her return ticket and her passport. The return ticket had expired and so had her travel insurance. She had her credit card and some traveler's cheques. She smiled as she ripped up her return ticket and threw it in the bin.

The next day, a chill descended in the air, and the atmosphere changed in the beach house. Ted introduced her to a friend of his called John; she took one look at him and felt really uncomfortable. He was skinny, with long limp hair and a goatee. He was a roofer. She saw Ted arguing with him out on the beach. It seemed heated. As the afternoon turned to evening, more friends of Ted's arrived. There was plenty of beer, and it wasn't long before several joints were being rolled. Sammy was offered a joint, and after the beer she had been drinking, she foolishly took some. The room began to spin as people's faces distorted in front of her. She wasn't sure what she had been given, but she felt sick and excused herself.

She lay down on the bed, and after what seemed like minutes, she felt her cut-offs being pulled down. She wanted to move, but she was temporarily unable to. She looked down to see John pull her shorts off. He was not alone.

Sammy struggled to move. She tried to say no, but it was impossible. She felt the heat of a mouth on her stomach as her legs were parted and then nothing. Rohypnol had taken over.

She awoke a day later in the same room. Her head was throbbing and she felt sick. She was naked. She began to panic as she tried to remember what had happened. Her head was foggy as she barely recalled the rape. She managed to get her clothes on and walked into the lounge. She was disgusted at what she saw. John was sitting in the chair grinning, holding a video camera. Ted was nowhere to be seen.

'You look great, Sammy, so photogenic. I will treasure this,' he laughed. 'Get your things and get out,' he said as he idly rolled a joint.

'You bastard!' she stammered as she frantically looked for the hire car keys. 'I am going to the police.'

'You do that and I will cut your throat. Now get your stuff and get out before I do.'
Sammy grabbed her bag, quickly checked for her keys, and fled out the door to where the car was. She turned the engine and drove towards Tampa airport in a blind panic. As she approached Tampa, the fuel indicator started to flash. She was low on gas. Pulling into a gas station, she reached for her bag. Her heart sank, and she had a massive panic attack—her passport and credit card were missing. Fighting for breath in the gas station, her legs hardly holding her up, the full shock of what had just happened hit her. A man stopped to help her. She started to scream.

'It's OK, ma'am. You will be OK. I have called an ambulance for you.'

She heard the sirens and then saw the sidewalk hurtling up towards her face as she fainted.

The ambulance took her to Tampa Hospital, where she was given oxygen and a blood test. She slept for hours, and when the doctor came to see her, he told her she had been drugged. Traces of Rohypnol were found in her blood. She sat stunned for a moment until the doctor said, 'Where are you going to go now? Do you have money to pay for your medical treatment?'

Sammy had never been to hospital in America, and it dawned on her that there was no National Health Service and that her insurance cover had expired.

'How much do I owe?' she enquired.

'A thousand dollars,' the doctor replied.

'Oh my god, I don't have any money. I can't pay it.' She began to sob.

'It's OK, don't worry. I will have you taken to a mission. You will get food and shelter there.'

'What happened to the car?' she asked.

'The police had it towed back to the hire company.'

'OK,' she replied, relieved that at least it hadn't been stolen.

She was desperate and broken as she got into the taxi. The driver told her it was a free ride and dropped her at 'The Mission of God' in downtown Tampa. It was a pigsty. Her handbag was empty; she had left all her belongings in Treasure Island, and she only had the clothes on her back to her name.

'Sammy, I am here to help,' said the lady at the reception. 'Now, we want you to shower and then you can get some food, but before you do, we need you to pray.'

Sammy looked shocked. 'What?' she asked.

'Pray to the Lord for the shower and the food.'

Sammy didn't know how to pray. She looked confused as the lady led her into a dormitory. All around her were what can only be described as down-and-outs. They shuffled around, shoulders hunched, not making eye contact with anyone. Some were physically or mentally disabled, others had scars or disfigurements. Sammy had never been so frightened in her life. She was shown a bed and was given some blankets and a towel.

'The showers are in there.'

The lady pointed to a doorway.

Trance-like, Sammy walked into the shower. As she looked around her, she saw cockroaches scurry up the walls and floor, and to her horror, she saw strewn soiled sanitary towels on the floor. She wretched and vomited, just making it to the toilet on time. Her body wracked with each wretch, her eyes were swollen with tears, and she was totally exhausted. She showered and fell exhausted on to her bed; she tried to shut out the muffled sobs from the other occupants. She couldn't get to sleep and remembered that there was a five-hour time difference between Florida and the United Kingdom.

She walked to the nearest call box and dialed the operator, reversing the call charge. The only number she could recall was the office.

'Becky, its Sammy. Is William there?'

'God, Sammy, where on earth are you? I've been worried sick. There have been terrible rumors. Are you OK?' Becky sounded really worried.

'Becky, please just put him on the phone.'

'Hello,' he said dismissively.

'Dad, it's me. I am in terrible trouble. I have been raped, I am stranded in Florida, and I have no money or passport.' Sammy sobbed down the receiver as she hung desperately on to the phone for support.

His reply left her cold, 'You resigned from this company, Sammy. You can fuck off and hitch-hike around America, as far as I care!' The phone went dead.

She stood shaking from head to toe, not understanding what was happening to her. Her eyes glazed over, and she became hyper-vigilant with fear. Her father's words echoed in her head as she struggled to breathe. He had cruelly and deliberately cut her off; sheer terror gripped her as she sank to the floor.

Chapter Eleven

Suicide or Homicide

Sammy walked into the sea hoping to drown herself. The waves crashed over her head as she tried to force herself under the water. She felt the air leaving her lungs and heard a piercing, high-pitched noise in her ears. She was pulled by the current out to sea. She thought about her brother, she thought about Four, and she thought about Number Two. She couldn't bring herself to go through with it. It was a sin, an act of failure, an act of a coward. The conversation with the vicar and the paranormal happenings at Oxleys Hall had made her think twice. She wanted to die, to put an end to her pain, but death could have been more painful than life. Would she cross over? Or would she remain between the two worlds as a poltergeist with unfinished business?

She didn't really know what she was going to do. She went to a police station to ask for some help. They told her that she needed to go to the British Embassy in Tampa. She was interviewed by a woman called Vivienne at the Embassy, who then phoned the company to talk to her father. He had a brief conversation with her and then hung up. Vivienne told her that he had said, 'I am sick and tired of her. She has tried my patience.'

Sammy was dismayed and asked what she should do. Vivienne told her there was nothing she could do. They couldn't issue an emergency passport without verifying who she was. Her next of kin had to identify her to the authorities, and her father had refused to. She didn't have enough money to buy a ticket. She was stranded.

Sammy lost touch with reality, walking around with no shoes, blistered feet, dirty and unkempt. She went back to the mission, which was unisex, but she was terrified of the men in there. She couldn't make any eye contact with them and was very watchful as she was expecting to be attacked again at any moment. She kept herself to herself. The other women in there all had tales of neglect and abuse, and she felt the deepest empathy for them. They were alone, scared, and unloved too.

She felt the need to keep moving. She went to Tampa Airport by train with a little money that was given to her by the others in the mission. She decided that she would make a plea at the airport to get the first plane back to the United Kingdom. She went to the airport information desk and told them what had happened. The staff there told her that she had to have a passport before she could fly home. However, in order to get an emergency passport, she had to have an airline ticket. She couldn't afford a ticket. Her distress obviously concerned them, and the manager of the airport called the manager of the Marriott Hotel on site. He generously provided her with a room and some food for free and told her she could stay there for a few days whilst she tried to sort out her predicament.

She was allowed to use the phone in the hotel; she again contacted the office, but her father refused to take her calls. Mrs Jones, his secretary, simply said, 'Mr Davis is not available' every time she called.

Whilst staying in the Marriott Hotel, she contacted Barclaycard and told them what had happened. They agreed to wire her some money. They were sympathetic and arranged for the card that had been stolen to be cancelled. She continued to want to keep moving but did not know what to do or how she should help herself.

She remembered Simon and Claire in Miami. Maybe they could help her? She thought she remembered where Mickey lived, but she had lost all track of time, and her memory was severely impaired. She was suffering from post-traumatic stress.

It was early February. She was extremely scared of everyone and paranoid. She took the train and found a Salvation Army hostel near Miami Beach, where she was given a bed. She was filthy, dirty, and had lost another stone in weight. The hostel was full and again unisex. She stayed at the hostel for just under two weeks trying to remember where in Coconut Grove Mickey lived. The regime there was up at dawn, breakfast, and then out to beg until early afternoon, then she was allowed back in to eat and sleep.

She spent the time during the day on the beach looking out to sea, haunted by her history, terrified of the present, and not daring to think about the future. She could not get a job as she needed a green card, and she was too scared to talk to anyone. She finally tracked Mickey down when she remembered his surname and looked him up in the phone book. She walked to Coconut Grove and knocked on his door.

'Oh my god, what happened to you? Ted called weeks ago and said you just took off.' He looked amazed to see her.

'I have been robbed. I need a passport and money to get home. Can you help me please?' she begged.

'Of course, come in. I am going to call Simon and Claire. The bathroom is, oh you know where it is. Go and get freshened up, Sammy.' Mickey tried hard not to show the look of shock on his face.

After the intervention of the Florida police and the British Embassy, Mrs. Jones confirmed her identity and paid for a ticket for her to get home. Detective Christopher of Metro Dade Police interviewed Sammy regarding the rape, but she was too distressed to make a formal statement. She just wanted to get home. The Consulate issued an emergency passport and she boarded Virgin Airlines at Miami Airport. She landed in Heathrow ten weeks after flying out for her vacation, more traumatised than when she had left.

She was still in deep shock. Claire had given her some clothes but she had no underwear and was very self-conscious, her feet were still blistered, her hip still painful, but her heart was shattered and her faith in humanity broken. Her physical scars would heal, but the mental scars would stay with her for the rest of her life. She had never relied on her father; she had historically held her own, financed herself, and lived an independent life. This had been the only time she had ever asked him for anything, ever. She had told him that she was in trouble, and he had inexcusably let her down. He was her only family. She had no uncles, no brothers or sisters, no mother, just him, and she could not comprehend how cruel he was in her time of need. Sammy wouldn't treat anyone like he had treated her. She would help a stranger; she helped people all of her life to the best of her ability. She could not comprehend his behaviour. What kind of man leaves his only daughter raped and stranded abroad for two months? What kind of man refuses to speak to the authorities about his own child? But there again, what kind of man is it that causes the suicides of his son and his wife?

She boarded the train back home and sat motionless, looking out of the window; England had never looked so good to her. It began to rain as the tears slid down her cheeks. What had she done to deserve this treatment? She couldn't help but internalise the feelings. Was she such an awful person? Had she been punished for something she had done or failed to do? The darkest depression hung over her like a thick cloak of death. She was locked in a cocoon of rage, doubt, agonising rejection, and fear. What she had escaped from was hell on earth. What she was returning to was just as bad.

She hadn't got her house keys or her mobile phone. She had to walk from the station the two miles home. She walked ghost-like up the hill to Oxleys Hall. Turning into her drive, she shuddered. Lionel jumped at her from the walled gardens, and she caught him in her arms, burying her face in his thick, soft black fur.

She got the key from the neighbour, who was inquisitive; she feigned tiredness and made her excuses, quickly leaving. As she pushed the door open, a mass of post blocked her way. She walked over it and into the kitchen. She pulled Lionel closer as he purred in delight to see her, and she smelt his familiar scent on her skin. She sat frozen in the kitchen as the sun faded and darkness descended.

As daylight broke over the fields, she emptied her change jar. She walked to the shop to buy milk and cat food. She returned home and called her doctor. The appointment was made for that afternoon. She laughed when she described to him what happened. Her laughter was a defence mechanism. She was diagnosed with post-traumatic stress and given medication. She went to have herself tested for pregnancy and HIV; fortunately, she was not pregnant or diseased in any way. The doctor gave her a sick note, and she was immediately entitled to Incapacity Benefit. It was a pittance, but she had nothing.

Her post was piled up by the door, so she attempted to go through it to see what was happening financially. She was three months in arrears with her mortgage and her utility payments and had been threatened with being repossessed and cut off by the utility companies. She was thousands overdrawn as there had been no money paid into her account. She remembered how her father had promised in Dr. Hatton's office to support her financially. She remembered how he had lied. She knew how he was a prolific liar; his lies hid his true nature.

Her clothes hung off her. She was under six stone in weight, her face was grey and drawn, her eyes haunted, she was losing her hair, but she carried on. She began to fight back, slowly. She considered making a claim under her travel insurance, however, once she had the form in front of her she could not bring herself to complete it as she wanted to block out the terrible ordeal she had been through. She found herself turning to alcohol to deaden the pain. Her mental state was such that she had to control overwhelming homicidal leanings towards her father. She had to physically and mentally stop herself from going to his office and killing him. The feeling was so hard to suppress; she planned how to kill him. She would take a hammer and batter his head. Her rage was almost uncontrollable; she had never felt so much hatred and anger in her life. She hated him for her brothers' suicide, she hated him for Number Two's alcoholic suicide, and she hated him for Four's suicide. She wanted justice. Someone had to teach this man a lesson. Someone had to make him take a look in the mirror.

She felt so used. She felt that her father had used her by asking her to resign as a police officer, sought her support whilst he regained his health, found a new interest in various women, and then thrown her aside. He had not considered what she had given up financially and vocationally to be at his side after his heart attack. Her father was not capable of loving her, and that is all she had ever wanted from him, not money, not position, just love. The feelings that she was left with were crippling.

She decided to confront him; she took the hammer from the toolbox and walked to the offices. With every step, she envisioned the first blow to his head; she visualised how the scene would play out in her mind. The hammer crashing down on his left temple, the thud on his skin, the twisted look of horror and pain as the blood seeped down his face, she swung the hammer again, harder this time, in the same spot as the flesh split open. Blood splattered the walls as he screamed in agony. She struck him again as his brain became exposed and he slid to the floor. She watched him lying there in agony and smiled to herself. 'Do you feel that? Do you feel the pain? You dish out nothing but pain. You are a manipulating, arrogant arsehole, and I hate you. This is for my brother and Mom!' With that, she kicked him with full force straight in the face, splitting his lip and breaking his nose. He cried out in agony as she smiled in twisted psychotic delight. His eyes rolled into the back of his head. 'Say sorry, you bastard,' she screamed as the blood and flesh hung off the hammer in her hand. 'Fucking say sorry, you bastard!' she screamed at him. He fought for his last breath and lay motionless on the floor.

The vision left her. She felt the hammer in her pocket as she flung the office door open. Mrs. Jones turned white and fled into the toilets, and she heard the door lock.

'Fucking coward!' she screamed at the doorway. She would deal with her later; she wanted to see her father first.

'You piece of shit!' the foreman said as she walked further into the offices. 'You are a piece of shit for what you have done to your father!' he said.

Her right fist rose in a flash as she punched him straight in the face.

'How dare you! Where is he?'

'Sammy!' her father bellowed.

She turned and looked at him. His face was scarlet. His eyes were furious as he stood in front of her.

'Calm down,' he commanded.

She swung the hammer out of her pocket and raised it. She glared at him. She wanted so badly to swing that hammer into his skull, but she knew in her heart that it was wrong. She knew in that instant of confrontation that violence was not the way; she had been pushed to her limit, to the very edge. Did he want her to kill herself? Did the ghosts of her past want her to kill him? This was insane. 'You bastard, you left me stranded out there. I could have been murdered. Where the fuck were you? I hate you. I will never forgive you. Where's my wages? I am selling my shares. See you in court!'

She let the hammer fall from her hand and turned away. She had at the final moment chosen the right path. She had a fight on her hands. She still owned 49 per cent of the shares. He knew that. It became clear to her why he hadn't wished her to come back, why he had wished her harm. It was all about the shareholding, not her or their relationship. The shares were all he cared about.

Now she had leverage. Now she could play him back at his own game. She had lost her mind momentarily, but in those psychotic seconds, she gained perfect clarity of the situation. Her brother had been a major shareholder when he committed suicide, and Four would have taken half of her father's assets on divorce. Sammy knew the truth. He had killed both of them for his business; he had murdered both of them for his greed.

She had lost her car, her income, her mind, the roof over her head was in jeopardy, and she had been cut off, but she had her shares in the company. It was hers, and the only way he could get them would have been upon her death. He would have automatically inherited. She smiled to herself as she walked out of the office and home; the shares were worth around two million pounds. She now had options. She had regained some power.

She walked head held high away from the offices, relieved that she had not committed murder. She had looked him in the eye and told him how she felt. The confrontation left her feeling calmer, more reasoned, more focused. She knew now what to do; she wanted to pay him back, to mirror him, to make him see what he had done, and how he had behaved.

Chapter Twelve

Betrayal

Her rational brain slowly began to take over. She thought carefully about how to play him at his own game. She wanted to hurt him, and the only way was to take money from him.

She telephoned his accountant, 'It's Sammy. I need a valuation for my shares immediately. I am selling them to the competition. Please call me back as soon as possible with a figure. Goodbye.'

She knew that he would call her father right away, and it wasn't ten minutes before her phone rang. 'How much do you want?' the accountant asked.

'Well, considering I am about to lose my house, have no car, and am in thousands of pounds of debt, half a million will do for now, or I am selling to the competition and going to the press.'

'I will be over this afternoon with a cheque. It won't be half a million, Sammy, but it will get you out of difficulties for now. Don't contact the competition, not yet, and don't involve the press,' the accountant pleaded.

'I will see you later.' She hung up and dialed the largest competitor.

'May I speak with your commercial director? It is Sammy Davis.' She didn't need to say what company she was from. She was well known in the industry. She knew it only needed a couple of phone calls in the right places to set tongues wagging. She wasn't serious about selling, but she wanted word spread that she was. The last thing her father would want was to share his precious company.

'Good afternoon, I am selling my share-holding as soon as possible, and I wondered if you may be interested?' she asked.

'Yes, of course. We have always wanted to acquire some shares, Sammy'.

'How many are for sale?' asked the director.

'Forty-nine per cent,' she replied.

'How much do you want for them, and have you offered them to anyone else?' he asked.

'They are currently valued at two million, and yes, I am open to other offers. I will leave my number and perhaps you can get back to me.'
She smiled as she gave her mobile number and hung up.

She dialed another competitor and repeated the conversation. The gloves were off; the thought of her father's fury delighted her. She began to feel better, she ran a bath, and prepared for the accountant's arrival. He knocked on the door; she answered it with hatred in her eyes.

'Look, Sammy, there is no need for this. Here is a cheque for twenty thousand. That should get you out of trouble, surely. Your father wants you back at work. Just come back on Monday, and all will be forgotten. He has forgiven you.'

She barely managed to control herself as she took the cheque from him. 'He had forgiven her!' What kind of crap was he spreading about her now?

'Right, tell him I will see him Monday. Goodbye,' she lied.

She ushered him out the door and called a taxi. She went straight to the bank and paid the cheque in. She then went home and called her solicitor and ACAS. She lodged a formal complaint of constructive dismissal and began to write a log of all the previous months of altercations with her father. She wrote to her doctor asking for a full copy of her medical history. She contacted her mortgage provider and all her creditors and paid them in full. With what was left over, she bought a car. Being mobile again boosted her confidence enormously. A replacement mobile phone arrived, and she started to try to get back to some form of normality.

The Hall was quiet, and whatever or whoever had been haunting her had left. She no longer felt worried or scared; she was more focused than ever. She didn't go back to see Dr. Hatton as she wanted no involvement with anything or anyone to do with her father or the company.

Her door wasn't knocked on once; nobody came to see her. She didn't venture out and took to going to the twenty-four-hour supermarket late at night so she wouldn't bump into anyone. She needed to be alone.

By the end of March, she had completed her ACAS forms and had seen a solicitor. They told her that her father was refusing to speak with them and had instructed his solicitors. The games had begun; her solicitors had agreed to let her pay after the event as they had valued the company and knew it was worth four million. She had half the shares, so she was in a powerful position to negotiate. Her father's responses were exceptionally childish to both ACAS and her solicitors. Accusations of lateness, shoddy work, and drug and alcohol abuse were hurled at her. Her character was blackened by his staff, and outright lies were told. She had expected it and let it pass over her head. A date was set for an interlocutory hearing, and she steeled herself, knowing she would see him outside the courtroom.

Andy, her neighbor, came with her for moral support. She looked in amazement at her father as he acted concerned, telling Andy,

'Is she still mentally unhinged? Do look after her, won't you?'

She met with the barrister, who ushered her into a consultation room.

'It doesn't look good, Sammy. We have noted that it was over three months from your resignation to your lodging of a complaint with ACAS. You are unfortunately out of time for a constructive dismissal complaint, I am afraid,' he said, shaking his head.

'Oh no, you're joking. I was stranded in the United States, and the company wouldn't help me. Surely that's exceptional grounds. I couldn't have made a complaint any sooner!' she pleaded.

'The time limit is three months. You are out of time. I suggest we postpone this hearing and meet again with the solicitor to rethink as soon as possible.' The Barrister was adamant.

She felt sick, her stomach churned as her head ached. All her plans came crashing around her as she looked at the barrister in disbelief. They reconvened at her solicitor's office.

'There has to be something I can do. This is so unfair!' she sounded devastated.

'The only choice now is to sell your shares, Sammy. You have no money, no job, and you have to do something to help yourself. Sell your shares,' the solicitor said.

Sammy pondered on the thought. She hadn't wanted to part with her shares. She wanted to make him think she was selling to worry him, but now it looked like it had become a reality. It was the only bond between them. It was the last resort.

'We will write to him and ask him if he wants to purchase them from you. It's probably the best way forward. You are in no fit state to find work right now, and we can't take him to tribunal.' The solicitor sighed.

'If that's all I can do, then I suppose I have no choice,' she replied dismayed.

She drove home, desperately upset that the tribunal she had so wanted was not to be. What a cruel hand fate had dealt her again! Her energy levels stooped to an all-time low. She was losing her will to fight any longer.

She was offered two hundred thousand pounds for the shares although the company was worth four million as a going concern. The offer was not a realistic reflection of nearly half of the company's value. At that time, the turnover was over three million, and the post-tax profit was over three hundred and seventy thousand. The articles of association came to light via her father's solicitor, which stated she could not sell to an outsider and had to offer her shares back to the company directors. If she had not been in financial ruin as a direct result of her father's actions towards her, she would not have sold the shares. She sold them back to the company under duress in order to get out of financial difficulties. Sammy had no other choice. It was obvious that she was not welcome in her father's life any more. She had lost her father, her job, her security, her home, her mental health, and was completely heartbroken.

She received the first instalment almost immediately directly into her bank. She took care of all her debts. She invested the remainder of the money with the bank, withdrawing those funds as and when she needed them to continue the standard of living she was used to. She put the house back on the market. It was no longer home to her. It felt tainted. It sold in little under a month. She was finally free from Oxleys Hall and its ghosts.

Sammy rented a two-bedroom maisonette as she was severely depressed and didn't want to commit to purchasing a property as she was uncertain as to her future. She had difficulty coming to terms with what had happened; her nights were haunted by memories.

Suicide was a constant thought. She felt and looked awful and was told on many occasions that she looked ill by virtually everyone that she met. She felt that she was dead inside. She became almost totally withdrawn and did not want to think about what had happened or associate with anyone that she had known. She had changed and was not the same person.

She spent a lot of time in bed, never wanting to get up or get dressed or do anything. She saw her doctor on several occasions and attended counselling. She could not, however, bring herself to discuss what had happened in America.

She spent around six months virtually as a recluse, then plucked up the courage to take up a part-time job in the pub, but she only lasted two days because a customer tried to flirt with her. It triggered the rape, and she left immediately.

After she walked out of her job at the pub, she spent another year as a recluse, hardly ever venturing out of the flat. Sammy became unable to account for anything else she did during that time. Life was a blur. Her mental state was terrible.

She re-applied to the police, but she was not invited to an interview. She was rejected but did not receive an explanation for the specific reason. She really felt that re-joining the police force would have helped her combat her various mental health issues and would have given her a renewed purpose. She wanted to get back to feeling herself again and boost her very fragile confidence.

She moved to a different, smaller house in the summer of 1999 and signed up to a recruitment and temping agency. She started work temping as a receptionist initially on just over minimum wage. It was temporary contract work, which lasted no more than a few months. She found the work to be a big comedown from her previous existence as a director of a successful company. She kept herself to herself and did not socialize with any of the other staff. She was not comfortable being around other people. It was extremely difficult for her to be at work as she would react inappropriately to any adverse comments or constructive criticism. She had a strong feeling that she was abnormal, reminiscent of the feelings she had when she was a child at school with several step-parents. When the sales manager gave her a compliment, which on reflection was innocuous, she resigned, terrified that he may rape her. She left the agency and went to work at Next in the local town, but she would encounter people that she knew there from her past, which made her feel uncomfortable. She was not happy with her job compared to her previous positions in the police and as a director. Her father's housekeeper came into Next and saw Sammy; she wanted to hide but couldn't escape in time.

'Sammy, I don't work for your father any more. He's fired me. You were set up, you know. They set you up, you were followed. There has been talk that they had cameras put in your house. Sammy, I am so sorry. There was nothing anyone could do. They want you dead so they can take over the company,' She spurted out.

'Thanks for telling me, aren't you sleeping with my father any more, then? I heard he was paying your husband to look after his house in France so you two could have some time together. That makes you just as bad in my book. You know, when I employed you to look after his domestic needs, I didn't write sex down as one of your responsibilities. I don't want to know. You make me sick, all of you. You are as much a gold- digger as the rest of them. I heard your daughter is now working in the financial department. Is she sleeping with him too? Do you have little cosy threesomes? I am sure your husband is very proud of you both. Now do me a big favour and fuck off!'

The former housekeeper was speechless. Sammy glared at her. They were all the same—those horrible, shallow women. They all had pound signs in their eyes. Sammy had heard nothing but gossip, rumors, and lies from all of the women in her father's life. She didn't know what the truth was. She didn't care. It was a game to her now. She had seen too much of it. None of them had loved him. It made her feel incredibly sad. Sammy had loved her father, but he was incapable of loving her in return. His love of sex, money, and position had turned him into a shallow, cruel manipulator. They all deserved each other. Sammy would never have fitted into his life. She was very much a square peg in a round hole; she cared little about designer labels or status. She was pleased she had been given the opportunity to change her life, albeit a hard departure. She had been hurt, but she had learnt a lesson.

Sammy felt absolutely nothing. She was numb. She had known all along that his life revolved around money and sex and just how evil he was. She didn't care. She was sick of the drama. Let them have it. She would make her own way in life. She finished her work and resigned immediately.

She was sick of her father's employees perpetuating her family history. She wanted to go where no one would know her, but where could she go to? She was too scared to dare move out of her home town, too scared of life to live, too frightened of death to die.

CHAPTER THIRTEEN

Congruence

January 2000 was bitterly cold. She shivered in her small un-heated flat. It was a rental on the outskirts of town, just big enough for her and Lionel. The rent wasn't cheap, and the bills were just about affordable. She enrolled on a counselling course at the local college and began to read vast amounts of books. She devoured them with a hunger for knowledge and a yearning for explanation. She remained calm on her classes, holding in her rage, trying to stop the pain from showing on her face. She was pleasant to her peers and tutor but remained aloof. Listening to her peers speak of their love for their families and children was hard to hear. She knew that she was different and knew how people would react if she dared to speak the truth. She once again excelled and was told by her tutor that she was well ahead of the class, with an exceptional innate understanding of her chosen subject. The coursework was fairly difficult, and writing journals about her deepest feelings was painful but cathartic. The reading lists she was given were an inspiration to her. She grew emotionally, her life dominated by study and self-discipline. The first year passed quickly and she felt focused. She read enormous amounts on suicide, grief, and emotional bonds. She studied humanistic, psychodynamic, and person centred counselling, and she counselled herself. She analysed her every thought, she investigated her own personal history, and discovered a new self. She began to self-actualise.

She didn't miss her old life. She rarely drank alcohol and didn't go out much. The drama she endured in her father's realm had all but faded. Life without him was wonderful. She no longer had access to the material things in life her former jobs had provided. She was living on a shoestring, but the freedom she felt was priceless.

There had been no romance or love interest in her life for many years. She did feel lonely, but she still harboured a hatred for everyone in her fathers' life. Few had shown her any kindness, and she distrusted them. Her studies had shown her the reason why.

Self-reflection was a large part of her studies and she revelled in it. She learnt that it was often the case that people projected themselves upon her. She began to realise that she had been very confident and intelligent before her illness, and that had caused envy amongst her associates, stepmothers, and also her father. She understood that he couldn't bear to think that she was independent and didn't really need him, so he had created an environment to make her dependent on him. He attempted to squash her self-esteem and make her a dependant so he could control her and make himself feel better. He was a controlling individual, and in his world, he was the boss. She had defied his wishes purely by not needing him. Outwardly, he had played the proud father to his associates, but his real game was much more sinister. She had been about to be promoted when he brought a swift end to her police career. He knew this and had maliciously used her good nature to entice her back to his realm. As his control drama became clearer to her, she despised him even more.

In 2001, her diploma was going well and she became very knowledgeable. Her tutors were impressed and had told her that when she had completed her training, they wanted her to become a teacher at the college. She was over the moon. She had come a long way since America. You would never have guessed what had happened to her. There was no trace of her illness in her behaviour or her demeanour.

Lionel became very ill, and she had to have him put down. She cried herself to sleep and missed her faithful friend immensely. She took his ashes up to Oxleys Hall, where she thought he had had his best times running around the fields and laid his ashes to rest under his favourite bush. The Old Hall looked beautiful in the summer sun. There were three out of the twelve houses up for sale. She smiled to herself. Were the poltergeists still running rampage? Or had she been completely psychotic? She would perhaps never know the truth. She would take out the positive and leave the negative behind. What had occurred in that house had been for a reason. She had come out of it stronger, wiser, and free.

Ironically, she missed her father. It was something that she couldn't understand. He was a psychological abuser, a murderer, and a hard-faced bastard, so how could this be? As with most abuse victims, it was all she had known. In psychological terms, she had been subjected to negative stroking from him. It would take years of positive stroking to undo the damage.

Her new-found knowledge had to be put into practice, so she decided it was time to see him again. All the women in his life had stroked his ego, flattered him, been subservient, and he had basked in it. Why had they done it? For his money, of course, no other reason. He was not attractive in the least. He was a short, fat, grey-haired, red-faced, ugly man by all accounts. They had manipulated him in the same way that he had manipulated them. It was axiomatic. It was comical.

Armed with her new knowledge, she called him at the office and played her trump card. 'Dad, I am so scared. Everything has been awful without you. I can't cope. I miss you so much. I need you to help me,' she nearly choked as the lies poured out of her mouth.

'Sammy, you better come to the office,' he replied flatly.

Sammy smirked. 'Bingo!' It would be like taking candy from a baby. She drove to the office in her second-hand car and her oldest clothes. She purposely looked a mess.

'Good grief, you look awful! Are you eating? Put some weight on, for goodness' sake,' he sighed with disappointment.

'I can't afford to eat, Dad. I was so wrong to ever leave the company. I didn't realise how much you did for me. I am so sorry. I have missed you so much.' She held the vomit in as she hugged him.

'Why are you driving an old car? Where are you living?' he asked.

'I can't afford a new car any more. I live in a little flat in town, but it gets so cold. I have no heating.' She coughed and batted her eyelids at him. She hated herself for playing the game, but everyone else used him for money. Why shouldn't she?

'That's awful. Let's get you stable. Find yourself a house and a car, and I will organise it for you.' He beamed with delight at her mocked show of dependence and neediness.

Within six weeks, he had bought her a detached house, a new car, and was giving her money on a regular basis. It was so easy. They met for dinner every week, and their relationship was reborn. She had regained what she had lost and was now financially stable. History repeated itself. Their relationship was exactly the same as previously. They did not speak of her brother, her illness, or America; they were taboo subjects. Thursday night was their night to meet and have dinner, and she would play the victim so he could think he was in control.

As they ate their meal, he said, 'Anne, or Number Five, should I say, and I are no longer together. She is fighting me for the house in France. She was trying to control me and nobody controls me!'

Sammy nearly choked on her potatoes. She so wanted to laugh out loud. The words 'I told you so!' were fighting to escape out of her potato-filled mouth. Her eyes started to water as she gulped them down and said,

'Oh, dear, I am sorry. You must be very upset.'

'Well, it's her loss, and anyway, Jane told me all about her scheming plans. She was after my money, you know. She was seeing other richer men all along, and she stole the product formulations from the office and tried to sell them to our direct competitors!' He scowled.

Sammy was biting her bottom lip to stem the hysterical laughter that was building up inside her.

'Oh, how awful! And I thought she loved you.'

'Well, I can tell you something. Jane is a godsend. If it wasn't for her, I would have never known. She is a lovely young woman.'

'Oh no!' thought Sammy. 'Please, no. Surely he can't be that stupid not to see their game. It was good cop/bad cop!' She looked at him and questioned,

'And how is Jane?'

'Well, you know how these things can happen. She is such a lovely young thing. Her daughter is so sweet too. Ahem, they moved in last week.' He gazed out of the window.

Sammy didn't know whether to laugh or cry, but the noticeable difference was that she didn't care. She had emotionally detached herself from him and his relationships. Her motive for reconciling was purely financial.

'Jane is doing some shopping for your new house, and we have some furniture for you. She will be coming round tomorrow. Now I don't want any of this jealousy nonsense, Sammy. Let's all get on and be a family, shall we?' He finished his gin and tonic and put his hand in his pocket,

'Are you all right for money?'

'No, Dad, I am a little short,' she lied.

He took out two fifty-pound notes and handed them to her. 'Right, I am off to meet Max at the Casino. Be good and I will see you next Thursday.' He kissed her on the head, and they walked to the car park. He got into his Aston Martin and waved as he pulled away.

Sammy got into her new car and drove back to her new detached home. 'Another game, another tart, another stepsister, nothing ever changes,' she thought as she got into bed and picked up her book. She would spend the evening with Freud; he was much better company than her father.

The phone rang. It was Sue from her diploma course.

'How did it go?' she asked.

'OK, I guess. He is seeing Jane now, so welcome to Number Six!' She burst out laughing.

'Jesus, what a prick!' Sue laughed.

'Play your cards right, Sue, and you could be Number Seven.' She laughed. 'But then again, you are too old, mate!'

'Are you coming out tomorrow to the bar? Come on, Sammy, you have to get back out there. You haven't been out for years. You are only thirty-two. Don't let life pass you by any more. There are loads of hot men out there. Please come. I could use the support.'

'All right then, I will. What time do you start?' she asked.

'Six, I will meet you there. Oh and dress up. It's quite posh in there,' Sue suggested.

'OK then. I will need a drink tomorrow. Number Six is coming over. See you at six.'

Sammy smiled as she hung up. She was looking forward to socializing again. It had been years, and she needed to boost her confidence and meet people. Sue was single and had started behind the bar. She seemed to like it, and it was a good stepping stone back to socialising. The bar in question was in a very affluent area and only five minutes from home. She would take a taxi and have a drink. She was, as Sue had pointed out, still only young, and it might be nice to have a love interest again. Her heart was still damaged and needed a lot of love to repair it; it was a risk she was ready to take.

The September sun was bright in the sky, a chill was in the air, and the colours were gorgeous. It had been five years since her fall into depression and subsequent breakdown. There were slight traces of it still in her. She stuttered occasionally, and her words often came out somewhat incoherently. She was still underweight and unnerved by the opposite sex. Her diploma course was totally populated by women, so it was easy. She shopped mainly online so she wouldn't bump into anyone; she was still hiding from her past, the rumours, and malicious gossip. It was time to face her judges. She had become strong enough. The past five years had been a journey she would never forget. She had gone from riches to rags, from sanity to insanity, and from love to hate. She had been abused, assaulted, used, and bullied. She had thought she would never pick herself up again.

Fortunately, her fighting spirit had prevailed and she felt ready to rise again from the ashes.

She began to strip the wallpaper as flashes of Oxleys Hall shot through her mind. She smiled as the paper fell on the floor, she lost herself in her thoughts. She was safe from harm. The house was in trust, but her father had promised it was for her to live in. She would never have to face the bailiff again. The radio was on as she climbed down the stepladders and put the kettle on. She had really got into chill-out music. The best thing about it was that there were rarely lyrics. She was moved immensely by music and often found lyrics to be relevant to her life, which would reduce her to tears. Chill-out was non-emotive for her and made her feel light and calm.

The doorbell rang and she opened it. She hadn't made an effort and was standing in cut-off shorts and vest, her hair pulled into a ponytail, bare feet, and paint splashed all over her.

Jane stood at the door carting a large box. Her car boot was still open and her daughter stood at her side.

'Come in,' invited Sammy.

Jane was still very fat. Sammy thought that she could use a gastric band, she must be putting a lot of booze away to have the nerve to sleep with a man older than her own father, the thought disgusted her. She was obese in comparison to Sammy. She recalled she had only met her twice before, initially with Anne and secondly at Oxleys Hall in 1996. There had been a couple of phone calls where she had accused Sammy of trespassing at her father's house. 'Here we go again,' thought Sammy.

'Your father asked me to drop this round. There's more in the car. Claire will help get them out,' Jane literally spat the words out. Her face was like thunder. If looks could have killed, Sammy would have been as dead as a dodo.

Sammy looked at Claire and noticed how big her ears were. As she eyed them both, visions of all five previous families came into her mind. It was impossible not to compare. They all had similar traits—big breasts. She wondered if Claire was being groomed for abuse. She must have been around seven. All his exes had daughters, apart from Anne who had a son. How strange that her father, who in her opinion bought and paid for his women, would always opt for those with children. Were young children a prerequisite for his attentions?

'Thank you for bringing it over,' Sammy replied nonchalantly.

'I am not staying. Claire and I are busy.' She placed the bags in the kitchen and walked out.

'Is that your new car?' Jane enquired, her face flushed with hostility.

'Yes,' replied Sammy.

'Huh!' Jane threw her head in the air as she stomped back to her car.

Sammy couldn't help but giggle as she closed the door behind her. What a bitch! She turned the radio up full blast and carried on stripping the paper. She was looking forward to going to the bar. At five o'clock, she ran a bath and soaked the paint of her. She washed her hair and applied moisturiser.

She relished the feeling of getting ready. It was all part of the night out. She dressed in smart trousers, she was still uncomfortable in skirts, and put on a fitted top. She styled her hair and straightened it. Putting on her make-up, she looked for traces in her face of the past. There were none. She stared at her reflection and was still surprised at her figure. She was skinny, but she liked it. The last appendage were her heels; she strapped them on and called a cab. Nervously waiting for it, she began to recall her nights out partying in her teens and early twenties and breathed deeply. She told herself to stay calm. She could do this.

The cab arrived and she smiled at the driver. She was still nervous and told herself over and over again that nothing would happen; she was in her home town with a reputable taxi company. She made no conversation with the driver; she looked pensively out of the window.

Sue grinned at her as she walked into the bar. Sammy found the nearest seat in the corner with a good view of the door and ordered a Jack Daniels. She felt the warmth of the alcohol in her stomach and instantly felt calmer. She smiled at Sue as they exchanged gossip over the bar. It was frequented by the locals mainly and most were professional businessmen, suited and booted. The car park was full of BMWs, Porches, Jaguars, and Audis. Sammy liked it. She remembered being the commercial director of the business and felt amongst equals again.

It wasn't long before Sue introduced her to a familiar-looking man the same age as her father. Sammy began to talk to him.

'I am sure I know you. Have I seen you at the Chamber of Commerce?'

'Yes, you are William's daughter, aren't you? How are you?' he enquired.

'I wonder what he has heard about me?' she wondered. 'Oh well, just go with the flow.'

'I am fine, thanks. I have taken a career break and am studying at the moment—psychology. Sue and I are at college together.'

'Yes, I know, Sammy. It's good to see you. How is William? Is he still with that awful woman?'

'Which one are you referring to?' Sammy laughed.

'What was her name now? The one who drove the Mercedes—bloody awful woman!'

'You are years behind, I am afraid. She killed herself years ago. He is on number six now. She is my age.'

'Good grief! When will he ever stop? Known him for twenty years or so. We played snooker at the Conservative Club. I hear the business is doing really well. Are you going back after your studies?'

'Who knows? Do you have children?' Sammy asked, desperately wanting to change the subject.

'Yes, my son works at the company with me. My daughter is married and a housewife. She's your age. We live next door to the bar, so I don't have to worry about driving home.'

'I got a taxi—better safe than sorry.'

The bar began to fill as an old school friend walked in.

'Hi, Guy. How are you?' Sammy smiled.

Guy was nice. He hadn't changed much over the years. He was a couple of years younger than she was.

'God, you have lost a lot of weight! How are you? Who are you with? My mates will be here in a bit. I will introduce you.'

'I am on my own really, but I came to see Sue behind the bar.'

'What do you want to drink?' grinned Guy.

'Jack Daniels.'

He got their drinks as they fell into conversation. Sammy felt relaxed and at home. It had been five years since she had been out, but it seemed refreshingly familiar.

'This is Mark,' said Guy.

'Hello, Mark. I am Sammy.'

'Pleased to meet you. Can I get you a drink?' Mark winked at her.

'Jack Daniels, please.'

The music was playing loud, the party people were dressed up and out to play, and Sammy felt good. She had been pensive for no reason. There was nothing to fear. She took the drink and began chatting to Mark and Guy. Sue was grinning at her from behind the bar.

'Do you want a line, Sammy?' asked Guy.

'What?' Sammy had no idea what he was talking about.

'A line of coke, you know, charlie?' He looked at her puzzled.

Cocaine, she understood what he had said. She looked at Mark and Guy and noticed how big their eyes were. She was feeling very drunk, but they seemed sober.

'You will be able to stay out longer. It will sober you up a bit,' added Mark.

'Why not?' she slurred.

Guy and Mark led her outside to Mark's Subaru and they got in. Guy pulled out a plastic bag from the glove compartment and his wallet. She watched as he tipped the white powder on a CD case and crushed it up with his credit card. He drew the powder into thick white lines and then rolled a twenty-pound note up tightly.

'Sniff it like this. Watch,' Mark said.

Guy held the case under Mark's nose as he lined up the end of the note on the line. Putting the other end to his nostril, he sniffed hard as the line disappeared up his nose.

Changing over with Guy, Mark held the case as Guy snorted the second line.

'Your turn.' Mark grinned, holding the case under her nose.

Sammy sniffed the line up her nose feeling it burn her nostrils and hit her brain like a torpedo.

'Wow!' she laughed as she felt wide awake. Her drunkenness faded as she felt alert and energetic.

Guy and Mark smiled as they passed the case round again.

Sammy laughed as she rolled up the note and snorted again. Christ, she liked the feeling. She started to dance to the music playing in the car.

She was as high as a kite. Thoughts of Jane and Claire vanished. She was having fun for the first time in years.

'Let's go back to yours and finish this lot. I'll stop at the off licence on the way and grab a bottle of JD. We can't go to mine. I live back at Mom's, and Mark's is miles away. OK?' Guy asked.

'Brilliant idea. Let's go. Just let me say bye to Sue.'

Sammy mouthed to Sue over the bar and waved.

Sue put her thumb up in agreement and grinned as Sammy walked back to the car.

Guy drove them to the off license, bought the Jack Daniels, and they laughed and sang all the way to her house, chatting nonsense.

Sammy put the stereo on loud, and the room filled with trance music as she poured the drinks. Guy and Mark tipped out a huge amount of white powder and racked it into white lines.

They sat chatting, drinking, and snorting till the sun came up. Sammy was trouble-free and began to seriously doubt the drug laws. How silly they seemed now! Had she been the odd one out all the time?

'You must have been the only one in this whole town that didn't snort coke, Sammy. Where have you been hiding?' asked Mark.

'God only knows,' she replied.

'Let your hair down, babe. Enjoy yourself!' said Guy.

Chapter Fourteen

Looking in the Mirror

Sammy's relief was enormous. To be financially stable again took some of her stress and anxiety away. She questioned her father's motives. He was now a multimillionaire and he boasted about it. He had probably only helped her out to be seen to be doing the right thing. Everything about him reeked of money—his Aston Martin, his designer handmade suits, his house in the country with a swimming pool, lake, and a snooker room. The worst appendage was his current woman; she was a nasty, conniving bitch. Sammy had struggled with the odd relationship with her biological mother and even more so with her stepmothers and her father's lovers.

She questioned her own behaviour and wondered if it was her own fault that the relationships were strained. She also questioned others she knew from divorced parents and found that it was a given. Relationships with parents and siblings could be difficult in their own right, but adding step-parents and step-siblings was tantamount to pouring fuel on a fire.

Most of her female peers seemed happily married and had or wanted children, but the thought of that to her was terrifying. It was the last thing she wanted. She made a decision to make it come to fruition. At her doctor's, she asked, 'Is it possible to be sterilised?'

'Yes, I will make you an appointment with the hospital, if you like,' Dr. Scott answered.

At the hospital, she was interviewed by a psychiatrist to ascertain her reasons for wanting the operation.

'You are aware that it is totally irreversible. You have no children. Are you sure you won't change your mind?' the psychiatrist asked.

'I am thirty-two, and I do not and never have wanted children. I don't want to use the pill any more, and this seems the most sensible thing to do to me,' Sammy responded.

'Why don't you want children? What about your parents? Don't they wish to be grandparents?'

Sammy howled with laughter as she looked the psychiatrist straight in the eye.

'Well, they made a real mess of being parents. There is no way I would ever willingly put a child anywhere near them.'

'That's a good enough reason. Sign this form, and we can get you booked in.' He laughed passing her the form.

The appointment was made, and she knew she had done the right thing. She couldn't wait to tell her father and see his face. Thursday night arrived, and she met her father in their usual restaurant. He was already in the bar drinking his usual gin and tonic. She smiled pleasantly at him and ordered a Jack Daniels.

'So how is your course going? Are you top of the class yet?' he questioned.

'It's going well, thank you. How's the business?' she asked in reply.

'Growing bigger every day, under my brilliance, of course!' he gloated.

'Still an arrogant prick, then,' Sammy thought as she got ready to pay him back a painful blow.

'I am being sterilised next month.' She looked him straight in the eye as she thought to herself, 'You fucking wanker, you will never get the opportunity to have your bloodline continue. You will never be a granddad. Your name dies with me.'

His face was an absolute picture as he stammered, 'What? Why on earth are you doing that for? Are you sure? Don't be ridiculous. Don't I get the opportunity to spoil my grandson?'

'I have never been so sure about anything. I don't want children. I never have. The operation is totally irreversible. I have made my mind up.' As she spoke, she thought, 'How completely selfish you are, you bastard. Who said it would be a boy? It's always been all about you, what you want.
You never cared for me. You only saw what you could get from me. You have no son. You will never get the chance to ruin someone else's life.'

'But what about my succession? What about the business?' he questioned.

'I haven't considered that. It's nothing to do with me anymore, is it? I don't work there.' She looked straight through him.

'You must reconsider, Sammy, really you must!' he implored.

'I have been studying emotional bonds recently and a lot of Freud's theories. Have you heard of the Oedipus complex?' she asked.

'No, why?' he replied.

'Perhaps you should look it up on the Internet. It's quite fascinating.' She watched closely as his face turned white. For the first time in their interactions, he was speechless.

Sammy felt a shift in power between them. She enjoyed seeing the distress on his face and knowing she had thwarted his plans. It was payback time now. She would mirror his actions exactly, and she would see how he liked being the recipient of such selfish behaviour. She had been rejected over and over again by him. Now it was her time to reject him. She wanted him to feel what she had felt. She finished off her drink and stood up; he was still eating his meal. She purposely said rudely, 'Must go, I am meeting someone. Bye.'

She would never normally display such bad table manners, but she wanted to leave him to think. She wanted him to know just how little she cared about him now. Her plan was to inflict just as much emotional pain on him as he had on her, no more, no less.

Mark and Guy arrived at her house and she had a great night. Guy's parents were divorced, and they swapped stories about step-parents. It was cathartic, and as the Jack Daniel's flowed and the cocaine took effect, she released her emotions in a safe and empathetic environment. Guy was acting almost as a client to her counselling acumen. She practised her counselling skills on him, and the sessions became real. 'Hadn't Freud used cocaine in his profession?' she thought. 'Damn right, he had, and who could blame him? He had actually prescribed it to his patients.' Guy hated his stepmother with a vengeance, and his father had died leaving him only bitterness. It was sad and Guy needed to open up. Their bond was founded on mutual pain and understanding. The drugs and alcohol were a crutch and a necessity for strength. She did question her use of both but didn't beat herself up about it. She had made an informed adult decision. She enjoyed recreational drugs. She enjoyed alcohol. It didn't interfere in her life, relationships, or work, so where was the harm?

That night, she wrote in her journal about the day's events and made a list of the things her father had done over the years that had hurt her. She would look for the opportunity to do the same. It wasn't out of malice. It was out of curiosity to see how he would respond and a sense of justice. She entitled her notes as empirical research.

The night before her operation, the telephone rang.

'Hello,' she answered.

'Sammy, are you sure about this? Listen, I have asked Jane to take you to the hospital in the morning and pick you up, but are you sure? You don't have to go, you know.' He sounded upset.

'I am going. It's what I want. What time is she coming? I had booked a taxi. I will be fine. She doesn't need to take me.' Sammy was delighted to hear him upset.

'I think it's best. She will be with you at seven. I will call you tomorrow.' He sighed as he put down the receiver.

'Does anyone ever consider what I want?' she thought as she got into bed.

Jane arrived in the morning with a face like a bulldog chewing a wasp. Sammy greeted her with about as much enthusiasm as a pig at a pig roast.

'You know he wants grandchildren. You are being selfish,' she hissed.

'Well, why don't you get knocked up, then, or are you still aborting yours? I think it better to take precautions before the event, don't you? Or maybe I could sell one like your mate!' Sammy smiled sweetly.

The operation was a success and she felt marvellous. She didn't have to worry about an unwanted pregnancy, and now she could be promiscuous. She was thirty-two. Good sex was something she had yet to discover, and she felt no guilt at all. Her reading list had opened her eyes. She found it amusing that for so long, men had been able to have guilt-free sex with as many women as they liked and were commended for it. She hated double standards. She had heard them boast, her father especially—about having mother and daughter, friends wives, younger women, married women, and sex workers. He wasn't the only one. They were all at it, so how could any man justify calling a female a slut or easy? Didn't women have just the same needs as men? It seemed women were oppressed by the very objects of their sexual desire. How ridiculous and archaic society was! She was not advocating that free love made a comeback, but she was not going to be bound by the societal norm or other people's expectations.

'I am going to Dubai for Christmas with Jane and Claire,' her father announced over dinner.

'How lovely for you all,' she flatly responded.

'I want you to come to my house for dinner next Thursday as we will be flying out the following week,' he instructed.

She, of course, wasn't invited on the holiday. 'Nice touch,' she thought. She would never have questioned it or indeed asked to be invited. The answer was a foregone conclusion, and she didn't need to hear it. She looked past him towards the car park. She didn't want to stay too long. Her usual Thursday night session was planned, and she was looking forward to seeing Guy and Mark. She had started to become attracted to Mark, and she knew he was having problems with his girlfriend. She ate her meal, made chit-chat, and then said her goodbyes. She had the taste of Jack Daniels in her mouth and couldn't wait to get wasted. Mark and Guy arrived punctually, and the scene was set for a night of putting the world to rights. The first line was good, really good. She felt the drug hit her brain and heighten her senses.

She smiled at Mark. 'How's things going then, now?'

'Awful, she wants a baby and I don't. I am too young.'

'Yes, you are. I wouldn't go there if I were you. They're expensive items to keep, you know!'

Guy burst out laughing. 'Cheer up, Mark. It could be worse. It could be me!'

They all laughed as the Jack Daniels and coke took them to a familiar state of consciousness.

'You seem to have it sussed, Sammy. Why can't she be sensible like you?

I just want to have some fun. I don't want to be tied down.' Mark looked forlorn.

'Ah, poor baby,' she mocked. 'Do you need a hug?'

'Yes, I do!' He smiled as he got up and put his arms around her. He felt good and he smelt delicious. Sammy put her arms around his neck as he turned his face towards her and kissed her full on the mouth.

'See you tomorrow then, Mark,' said Guy, grinning, as he let himself out the door.

'You are the prettiest thing I have ever seen. I have wanted to kiss you for so long. You're gorgeous,' Mark whispered in her ear. Their lips met once again as her pulsed raced. His lips were firm and soft, his tongue wet. He pulled her against him as his hand stroked her back; she ran her fingers through his thick brown hair.

'I want to fuck you. Let me fuck you,' Mark rasped.

She answered him by unzipping his fly and taking his erection in her hand. He moaned in pleasure. His hand grabbed her jumper as he pulled it over her head and buried his head in her breasts. His cock stood stiff and proud as his jeans fell to the floor. He stepped out of them and pulled her jeans down to her knees, exposing her black G-string and her toned legs. Still kissing him, she stepped out of her jeans as they moved to the desk in her study. He pushed her on top of the desk and spread her legs with one hand, pulling her G-string to one side with the other. She still had her high heels on, and she felt as sexy as hell spread eagled on her desk.

'Fucking hell, you're beautiful, Sammy. I am going to fuck you so hard.' He entered her slowly as she gasped for air. Still in her heels and G-string, she bent over the desk as he pulled her hair and fucked her from behind.

'Want a line?' she teased as she stood in front of him holding the rolled-up note.

They snorted till the small hours and drank the bottle of Jack Daniels.

'Let's go in the gym,' Sammy suggested. She had a multi-gym in her garage, and she had always fantasised about being fucked on the weight bench. She led him by the hand into the room and sat him on the bench. Pulling his trousers and pants to his knees, she straddled him and kissed him. His erection came back with a vengeance as she rode him using the arm press for balance and grip. She had fulfilled a fantasy. She was not surprised to find how much it had turned her on and how much Mark was impressed. She had learnt how to use her sexual power.

'You sexy bitch, can I see you tomorrow?'

'It is tomorrow,' she laughed.

On Thursday, she drove to her father's and knocked on the door. Jane answered it with Claire at her side. She looked like a shark defending her territory. She was obviously not happy with the arrangement. The kitchen table was laid, and Sammy was taken back to the other women who had claimed it as their territory—Number Four and Five. She hoped that Jane would meet a grisly end too. He had only lived there for eight years and had acquired three concubines in that short time. She worked out the average time span and wondered how long Jane would be around for. It was such a joke. Sammy instantly noticed that the professional photographs she had had taken for her father that used to be in the lounge were gone. In their place were pictures of Jane and Claire. The conversation at the dinner table was stilted; she really had nothing to say. Her father broke the silence.

'Jane and I want you to feel at home here. You look so much better now you are stable. Awful business, that American thing, well, that's all by the by now. Time to move on. You can come here anytime. Just make sure you call first.'

Her eyes hid the rage that had been ignited within her. How dare he glibly mention America and what had happened! He referred to it as though he had played no part in it. She wanted to punch him. He had no conscience whatsoever and no remorse. He had simply swept the incident under the carpet and wanted her to do the same. She would never forget it.

'Here's your Christmas present. We will see you in the New Year. We will be away for just over a month.' He handed her a card and as she opened it, the cheque fell out.

'How thoughtful! Just what I wanted,' she said.

'I got you guys a little something too.' She handed him a neatly wrapped box tied with a ribbon.

'Well, that's very nice of you, Sammy.'

She held the laughter in as he undid the gift. Pulling it out of its wrapping, he placed the box on the table and read the label, 'Happy Families, a board game for all the family.'

She passed him a look that said it all. Getting up from her chair, she said, 'Happy Christmas, Dad,' as she walked out.

'So what are you doing for Christmas?' asked Mark as they lay in bed the following evening.

'Nothing. Think it's going to be beans on toast for me again,' she replied.

'That's a bit crap, isn't it? I will come over on Boxing Day, if you like. I have to spend Christmas Day with my family,' he replied.

'Yes, I know. Most people do.' She grimaced at the thought.

She decided to treat herself that Christmas and bought herself a frozen chicken microwave dinner. On Christmas Day she sat and watched the television, periodically reading and sending text messages to Mark. She spent the day and evening totally bored and thought what a waste of time Christmas was. It was stressful, expensive, and bored her to tears. She didn't have an alcoholic drink or any drugs. Mark arrived early the next morning, and she asked him if he fancied a walk. She wanted to go her father's house to clear her head. It had several acres of land attached to it and was in the country, surrounded by woodland. Mark said he would follow her in his car as he had to visit other relatives later on. The garden could be accessed easily from the drive. Close by was a right of way for ramblers, and there was plenty of space to walk around in.

'Wow!' was the first word out of Mark's mouth. 'Did you live here?' he asked.

'No, I used to house-sit, though, when he was on holiday. I like the grounds. Come on, let's go for a walk.'

They walked to the side of the wooden bungalow and into the massive garden at the back. There was a lake at the rear with an old wooden boat.

'Let's go on the boat!' Mark enthused. He rowed them around the lake as she took in the scenery; it truly was a tranquil place, but she shuddered as she remembered Four taking her own life. The outbuilding that she had driven into to gas herself was still there. Sammy would have had it demolished. In fact, she would probably have sold up and left in the circumstances. She remembered the winter of 1996 and the poltergeist. Had it been Four? Was she trying to harm her or trying to tell her something? Pushing the thoughts far from her mind, she turned and looked at Mark. She really liked him. He was very handsome, but she knew he wasn't the one for her. He was too young and too immature. She would enjoy it while it lasted.

'I better go and see my folks,' he said.

'OK, I will see you out. Come on, we better put this boat back.' Walking up the hill towards the house, she noticed the bedroom window was open.

'That's not very wise, is it?' she said.

'No, better check the house,' he replied.

Sammy approached the bedroom patio doors and pulled the handle down; the door swung open. 'Better go in. You OK?' she said.

'Yes, after you. You were a copper, not me!' laughed Mark.

They entered the house and searched for signs of a break in. It was all secure. 'Must have just left the door open,' she concluded.

'I really have to go, Sammy. I will call you later,' Mark said as he kissed her goodbye.

'OK, I will just call the police because the alarm is on Redcare, and they are probably on their way,' she replied.

Mark drove away, and within minutes, a police car pulled on to the drive. Sammy opened the door with a big grin. She still loved to see the police; she had the utmost respect for them and missed her former occupation. She liked the opportunity to converse with the law.

'OK, it's a fair cop. It was me, Officer!' she grinned.

The police officer smiled. 'Tripped the alarm, have we, miss?'

'No, it's my father's house. I was just having a check up on it, and the window and door were left open. I came in and the alarm went off. Sorry to inconvenience you. Here's my driving licence for my identity.'

The officer checked her licence and said, 'That's fine, Sammy. I will have to call a Mrs Jones. She is listed as the keyholder. Do you know her?'

'Yes, it's my father's secretary. Tell her I am here and will be staying. I will set the alarm and lock up in the morning.' It was something she had done many times before.

'OK, goodbye. Have a good evening,' replied the officer as he turned and drove away.

Sammy got the key to the snooker room and let herself in. Floods of memories came back to her as she sat at the bar. She had hosted lots of parties in there in her twenties, and she remembered them fondly. It now seemed like a million years ago. She was surprised to see the snooker table covered over and an array of riding gear arranged on top. The fruit machine that she had gone to great lengths to find and buy for her father's birthday had gone from sight. She had come a long way and grown emotionally in the last couple of years, but it still hurt. She looked behind the bar and saw it was well stocked.

Taking a glass and a corkscrew off the shelf, she poured herself a large glass and sat thinking about where it had all gone wrong. One glass followed another; one bottle followed another as she heard a car pull on to the driveway. Mrs. Jones and her husband entered the snooker room. Sammy had not seen her for over five years. She didn't really know how to take her. Mrs. Jones eyed her with suspicion.

'Hi, Happy Christmas,' slurred Sammy.

'I thought I better come and see that everything was all right,' she said.

'Why? The police have already been. There is nothing wrong. They left the bungalow insecure. I have had a drink now and am staying. Didn't the police tell you?'

'Yes, but I still wanted to check everything was all right up here.'

'What did you think I would be up to? Don't tell me you actually believe what he tells you, do you? For god's sake, you came to all my parties in here. What's the problem? It's my father's house!' Sammy glared at them.

'We will be off then. Merry Christmas.'

As they left, Sammy felt utterly dismayed. In her view, she hadn't done anything wrong, so why was she treated with such contempt and suspicion? She went to what used to be referred to as her bedroom and got into bed.

Loud voices and banging on the patio doors to the bedroom awoke her. She was startled momentarily until she recollected where she was. 'What on earth was all the noise about?' she wondered. Pulling back the curtains, she saw the foreman and four of his cronies from the factory standing angrily at the door. She laughed to herself as she waved and pulled the curtains back.

'Open this door at once,' demanded the foreman.

'Just a minute.' She yawned. Putting her clothes on, she unlocked the patio door as all five rushed in.

'Where are they?' the foreman seethed, his face was bright red.

'Where's who?' she asked genuinely.

'I know you have got men in here. Lads, go and search the place,' he ordered. The four muppets he had brought along with him scurried off in different directions.

'I have told your father and he is fuming. You better get out!'

She couldn't believe it as he encroached into her personal space and forced her backwards out of the bedroom door. 'Oh, I see the game, is this payback for me getting shares and you not having any? Or is it payback for the time I punched you in the face? Is that why you brought some back up with you?' She laughed in his face. 'I was leaving anyway, and for your information, there is no one here, just me. I wouldn't disrespect my father's home. I will just get my bag from the kitchen.' She laughed in his ugly, twisted, red face.

Incredulously, his cronies had blocked her path from the hallway to the kitchen. 'Excuse me, my bag is in there with my car keys. If you want me to leave, I suggest you let me get my bag.' Her tone was mocking. They moved closer together and then walked towards her, forcing her backwards out the door on to the drive and slammed the door in her face. She stood dumbstruck for a moment, then the door opened and her bag and shoes were thrown at her. 'Well, how charming. It's good to be back,' she thought as she got into her car and drove home. She thought about it on the drive home. How could she ever attempt to achieve any stability in her relationships with people like that around her? Was it jealousy on their part? What had she done now? Surely she had not acted incorrectly in any way. What exactly was the problem with going to her father's house? She had keys to the place. She had house-sat and had parties there with his consent. Her behaviour was consistent, his was totally irrational. She was bewildered again.

CHAPTER FIFTEEN

Opportunity Knocks

It was New Year's Eve and she drove to the bar. Sue was working and the place was packed. Sammy felt incredibly sad. She had decided she would get a taxi home and leave the car. As the evening wore on, familiar faces came in, and she recognised an old friend of her stepmothers. He immediately came over.

'Hi, Sammy,' he slurred, 'Happy New Year!'

He was very drunk and leant in to kiss her cheek. She didn't like him and remembered how he used to boast openly about screwing Number Two's best friend and her teenage daughter.

'How's William? Is he here?' He looked around the bar.

'No, he's on holiday with his girlfriend and her daughter in Dubai.'

'Why didn't you go?' he enquired.

'I wasn't invited,' she replied.

'Man was a bloody idiot for ever leaving Chrissie. God, I miss her. She was such a lovely woman. Damn shame about your brother too. He was a lovely lad. Terrible business that suicide, just awful. Why did he do it, Sammy?'

She felt the vomit rise in her gullet and stared blankly at him. As she looked around the room, she saw happy families everywhere. She saw loving couples and good friends and wished the ground would swallow her whole. She had never felt so completely alone. A wave of grief swept over her as she gulped down her Jack Daniels. She wished he would shut up, but he carried on talking as his words cut her to shreds.

'I hear he has a young bit of totty with him now. He always said he would marry eight times, and the last one would be black, dirty old devil!' he laughed.

She couldn't bear to be in the room and listen any longer. She walked out of the bar with her heart aching and her thoughts racing. Foolishly, she got into the car and sped away. It was dark and icy; the country lanes were dangerous. She was driving too fast, desperate to get home, when she lost control of the car and it slammed into the curb. She was shaken but not hurt. She tried to restart the engine but it was dead. The tyres had burst, and there was fluid all over the road. She saw the blue lights behind her and watched as the police officers got out of the car.

'Hello, Chris.' She smiled as she recognised a former work colleague.

'Have you had a drink, Sammy?'

'Yes, are you going to bag me?' she asked.

'Have to. Sorry, mate, you know the procedure.'

She blew into the breathalyser, and it immediately went red. 'Sammy, I am sorry, but I have to arrest you.'

She sighed and got into the back of the police car. 'You stupid idiot!'she told herself.

In court, she pleaded guilty and was banned from driving. She accepted her punishment on the chin and sold her car. She would walk; she thought it would do her good. Mark and Guy were great about it after they stopped laughing. They gave her a lift wherever she wanted to go, and she discovered home delivery service from the supermarket. Her father returned from his holiday and telephoned her at home.

'What the hell do you think you are playing at? My foreman has told me all about it. Did you have men in my house?'

'What? No! I was in the house alone. What's the big deal?'

'I see you helped yourself to my wine, and Jane noticed there was food missing. How dare you! I wouldn't do that in your home,' he growled.

'I wish you would. You would be more than welcome. What's wrong with me eating some food? You are crazy. You tell me to make myself feel at home, and then you change your mind. What have I done wrong?' she asked.

'You didn't have my permission to go into the house,' he said coldly.

'What? Permission? Since when do I have to have permission to go to my own father's house? You are being ridiculous.'

'I will not tolerate your behaviour, Sammy. I never know what you'll get up to next.'

'I haven't got up to anything. It's normal for me to go to my parents' house. I have a key!'

'Well, I want it back. Jane doesn't want you nosing around her belongings.'

'I don't go through people's things. I found the door open. You had forgotten to lock it. I was acting in your interest. Who said I had men in there? That's a lie. I had friends in the snooker room, as I have done in the past with your consent. This is ridiculous.'

'Don't do it again, Sammy. Are we meeting for dinner on Thursday?' he asked.

'Not unless you pick me up. I have been done for drink drive. I am banned.'

'You stupid idiot, you, of all people, should know better!'

'Don't judge me. You were done too, remember.'

'That was different. I will pick you up then. No, I will come to you, and you can cook me a steak. See you at seven.' He put the phone down.

He arrived promptly and she invited him in. She was furious with him and they rowed.

'What is wrong with you? You are a control freak? You blow hot and cold and change the goal posts all the time. I can't cope with your behavior any more. You are driving me crazy!' she yelled at him.

'You are not my daughter, and I want a DNA test to prove it!'

'What!' she said completely dumbstruck.

'I never wanted you. You always stopped me from doing what I wanted. I should have put you up for adoption when I had the chance!'

'You never loved us, did you? You never told me or my brother that you loved us. You killed him, you bastard!'

'You tried to ruin my business, you ungrateful child. How could you?!'

'What? What are you talking about? I was ill and you didn't care less, you heartless pig!'

He walked towards the door. 'I am not listening to this.'

'Don't you dare walk away from me!'

He walked out the door, slamming it behind him.

She couldn't take in what he had said. How cruel could he be?! The thought that he would evict her crossed her mind and she shivered. She went to college in the morning and looked visibly ill. Sue noticed there was something wrong, and at coffee break, Sammy told her what had happened.

'What are you going to do?' she asked.

'I don't know. I just don't know. I am praying he doesn't kick me out.'

'Go and see him at work. I will give you a lift, if you like.'

'Thanks, Sue,' Sammy said.

On Monday, Sue picked her up and drove her to the office. Sammy knocked on his door and walked in. He looked distressed and very quietly said, 'The foreman died yesterday.'

'Oh,' she replied. 'Good!' she thought.

'I will let you know when the funeral is. I will call you later. I am really up to my eyes in work at the moment.'

'OK,' she said and walked back to the car.

She knew they needed to talk. She needed to clear the air and the past. She couldn't help but love her father, but she couldn't cope with being in his life. It was too erratic, and he was volatile. She walked on eggshells around him and hated their relationship. She was locked in a toxic relationship with him, but he was all she had. She prayed things could be different. She didn't know what to do, so she just waited for him to call.

He called three days later, 'The funeral is on Monday. I am not up for dinner tonight, Sammy,' he said.

'That's understandable. What about next week?'

'I will let you know.'

The following Monday lunchtime, her phone rang again and she answered it, 'Hello.'

'Where are you? I am at the crematorium,' her father said.

'I didn't say I was coming,' she replied.

Sammy had never liked the foreman and she certainly wouldn't be a hypocrite. He could rot in hell as far as she was concerned.

'I expected you to be here. Are you coming or not?' he asked.

'No,' she replied.

She made a mental note and ticked off one of the items on her list of things to pay him back for. He hadn't attended her twenty-first birthday party. She went back to reading her course books and became engrossed in her studies. She was glad the foreman was dead; she relished the thought of never having to see him again. Mark knocking at the door interrupted her. She was surprised to see him and answered the door with a smile.

'Hi, come in. You OK?' she asked.

'I have had a massive row with my father about my ex-girlfriend. She has been hassling me all week to get back together, and my mom and dad are furious with me for finishing with her,' he said sheepishly.

'It's your life, Mark. You're an adult. Are you still living back at your parents?' she asked.

'Yes, but they are driving me mad. Can I stay here for a while?' he asked.

'Course you can. That would be great!' she said.

They spent the rest of the day playing computer games and listening to music. Guy turned up later, and as usual, there was plenty of cocaine. The doorbell rang, and Sammy spotted a white BMW outside. She answered the door to a pretty-looking girl she hadn't seen before.

'Is Mark here?' the girl asked.

It dawned on Sammy that this was his ex-girlfriend. She felt uneasy. 'Hang on a minute,' she said as she closed the door and went into the lounge.

'Mark, your ex is outside.'

'You're joking!' He looked shocked.

'No, seriously, she's at the door.'

'Oh, shit! I will be back in a minute.' He walked to the door as Sammy and Guy looked at each other.

'How does she know where I live?' Sammy asked.

'I think she has been following him.'

'Oh, terrific,' Sammy sighed.

What was it with men's ex-girlfriends? Were they all psychos? How embarrassing! She heard the door close, and Mark walked back in with a scowl on his face.

'Nightmare, I don't believe it. She's followed me here. I am really sorry, Sammy.'

'Don't worry about it. How long were you together?' she asked.

'Two years. My mom and dad wanted us to get married.'

'I guess she is really upset then.'

'Yes, especially now I am taking the BMW back.'

'What's happening to your house?' asked Guy.

'It's rented, so she will have to move out. She can't afford to rent it by herself.'

They all continued chatting and Guy left at about eleven.

Mark and Sammy went to bed. It seemed strange having a man about the house again—strange but nice. The loud knocking on the door startled them, and Mark shot out of bed and looked out the window. 'Oh shit! It's my dad,' he said.

'You're a nightmare, Mark!' she laughed.

'Back in a bit.' He grinned.

'How odd,' she thought. 'Wasn't Mark a little too old to have his parents telling him what to do? He was twenty-eight, not eighteen. She, by contrast, had not had that trouble; her father hadn't taken the slightest bit of interest in any of her relationships.' Mark came back into the bedroom looking very solemn.

'Want to talk about it?' she asked.

'No,' was the reply.

Mark stayed for a month, and they got along really well. Guy was a regular visitor and even helped decorate and lay wooden floors. Half term was imminent, and Sammy fancied a holiday. She hadn't been anywhere since America and wondered if Mark wanted to go away.

'Do you want to go away somewhere for a week?'

'I would love to, but I can't afford it until I have sold the BMW.'

'I will pay. You can give me the money back later. Come on, it will be great!'

'OK, you're on. Let's book it online.'

They booked two weeks in Tenerife, flying out the next day. It was just what she needed.

The heat and smell hit her as she stepped off the plane. She smiled as she breathed in the sweet warm air and reached for Mark's hand. It was bliss. They had a fantastic time. They swam in the pool, walked hand in hand along the beach, he taught her how to play pool and cards, and she felt relaxed. Her only concern was the amount of times Mark talked about cocaine; he seemed to be unhealthily distracted by it whereas Sammy hadn't thought about it at all. One evening as they sat outside having a meal, he took her totally by surprise.

'Will you marry me?' he asked.

'You are kidding, right?' She laughed back.

'No, I am serious. If there was a vicar here, I would marry you right now.' As the words left his mouth, they both looked stunned as quite coincidentally, a man wearing full clerical attire walked past them.

'Oh my god, did you see that?' said Sammy.

'Spooky!' laughed Mark.

'I don't think we have known each other long enough really, Mark, but I am very flattered.' Sammy answered him.

'Yeah, OK, what about in two years' time, then?'

'We will see then,' Sammy said.

The fortnight passed quickly, and they returned home looking healthy and relaxed. Guy had house-sat whilst they were away and decorated the bedroom. It looked fantastic and she was thrilled.

'I am not going back to work. I am going into business with Guy,' Mark announced.

'Doing what?' Sammy asked.

'Buying and selling,' he said.

'Buying and selling what exactly?' she probed him.

'Cars and stuff,' he replied sheepishly. 'I have sold the BMW.'

Sammy was concerned but pushed her fears to one side. As she was about to leave for college, she was leaving Mark alone in the house. She said, 'What are you up to today?'

'Not a lot,' he said.

Sammy felt uneasy about leaving him in the house, and when she returned later that day, she found that her instinct had been right. Mark had two male friends at the house, and he was obviously as high as a kite. His nose had started to bleed, and he attempted to hide a very large package from her.

'What's that?' she questioned.

'I told you I was buying and selling. This is the first load. Who needs to do a nine to five? This will make me rich, Sammy,' he said.

'You lot, get that package out of my house now!' she ordered.

'What's wrong? Chill out, Sammy.'

'Get your stuff and get that shit out of my house right now! Mark, you stupid idiot, are you crazy? You could get seven to fourteen years in prison.

Get it out now!' she fumed.

She was furious with him. How disrespectful could he be?! How totally and utterly stupid he was to blow his job and his money on cocaine! She wanted no part in it. It was over between them. He was a fool.

CHAPTER SIXTEEN

Number Six

Sammy was disappointed with Mark. He called a few times and Guy relayed messages to her, but she wasn't interested. Recreational drugs were common in the neighbourhood, but she still felt uneasy around the scene. She had been a police officer, and it was something that didn't sit well with her at all. She didn't receive any of the holiday money back from Mark. Another lesson had been learnt. She curiously looked at Internet dating sites and signed up with one. It was a pleasant distraction from her studies, and she met several men and went on many dates, nothing serious. Sometimes she was attracted enough to have sex with them, other times not. She considered herself to have a mature attitude towards sex now, and the playground ethos was a thing of the past. She met and dated a bar manager in the city, and over dinner one night, he made her a job offer.

'Sammy, you have a presence about you. Would you work on the door as a female bouncer for me? It's fifteen pounds an hour, cash, and we could see more of each other?' he asked.

'Yes, I would love to,' she replied without hesitation.

It was an opportunity to get paid and be out all weekend in the thick of things. It suited her to the ground. She had loved being on the front line as a police officer, and her acquired skills and conflict management knowledge would be as asset. Her first night was brilliant. She laughed and joked with the patrons and searched the females. It was something she was quite used to. There was no trouble that night, and she met up with the manager at about 2.30 a.m. She had thoroughly enjoyed herself, and he gave her great feedback. 'You were great! The staff love you. Thanks, Sammy!' He handed over her wages.

She was thrilled. It was a great part-time job, and she could still study. Her social skills were coming back to her, and she found herself smiling again. She felt useful and she was earning a wage. Life was getting better. She worked on Thursday, Friday, and Saturday at the bar and also their sister nightclub. It was an extremely social position, and she also enjoyed the conflict and fighting. She was not in the least intimidated by violence and had brought out her latent physical intervention skills. She pleasantly shocked the male members of the team by administering control and restraint techniques when violence flared, and she quickly de-escalated potential risks.

'There is a course now for bouncers. The government have regulated the industry. You have to get a licence now. We all do. Here's the number of the training academy. You'd better book yourself in,' one of her colleagues told her.

The training academy was local, and she arrived expectantly in the classroom. It was a doddle, and she floored all the other pupils when they practiced control and restraint. She had found a use for her anger.

'Are there any jobs going here?' she asked the instructor.

'Well, yes. I could do with an assistant. Come back next Monday, and I will get you an interview with the boss.'

The boss was a big man, at least six foot two, and he had the look of a policeman.

'Hi. Let's have a look at your CV.' He studied it intensely and smiled. 'What nick were you based at? I was at Hurst St.'

She knew it. He was an ex-policeman. He introduced her to his business partner, and it transpired that he too was a former sergeant. She had found her niche.

'You are just what we are looking for, Sammy. When can you start? I will pay you cash. We will train you up to be an instructor,' he said.

'I can start tomorrow!' She smiled. This was the best thing that had happened in years. She was back on the career ladder. Her diploma could wait. She wanted to be back at work, and this job was just the ticket.

'See you tomorrow then. Welcome aboard!'

She went straight to college and swapped her class to the evening course. Getting a job was her priority. Her studies could be completed anytime. She would complete the third year, then put it on hold.

Her father was soon to be sixty-five. His relationship with Jane was continuing, and Sammy saw less and less of him. Losing her licence was the perfect excuse not to go for dinner, and at their more recent meetings, Jane and Claire had tagged along. Sammy saw no point in going. She couldn't stand Jane and would not pretend to like her for her father's sake. When in her company, Jane would drape herself across her father, and it made Sammy physically want to vomit. Jane was thirty-five, her father sixty-five. Sammy could not stomach it.

Sammy was invited to his birthday meal at the casino. Various members of staff would be attending and she was dreading it. She kept herself to herself and just watched the ensemble; it was the worst kind of company she could imagine. There were more brown-noses there than at a cattle market. Her father held court and Jane sat draped over him. It was disgusting. She wondered to herself how many of the female staff amongst them would he have been screwing. Probably all of them.

She just didn't have the will to make any conversation and felt like a spare part. She didn't like anyone in the room, let alone her father. Her father shared a taxi with her and dropped her home first and in his drunken state actually walked her to her front door.

'What's the matter, Sammy? My friends are all right, aren't they?' he questioned.

'Yes, Dad, I am just tired. Goodnight.'

She let herself in and went straight to the bathroom and threw up.

She settled into her new job with ease and impressed her boss. She was soon qualified to be an instructor and loved her work. She had never laughed so much in her life. The feedback she got from her students was awesome. She had to get a taxi to and from work, but it was worth it. She was gaining a good reputation for herself. As part of her training, she had to attend teacher training at college part-time, and she thoroughly enjoyed her learning and continued professional development. She still dated a few men, nothing serious. She was enjoying herself again and seemed to have come full circle. Then she received a phone call from a member of her father's staff.

'Sammy, your father has had a stroke and a heart attack. He is in hospital.'

Her heart leapt into her throat as a familiar feeling engulfed her. She called a taxi and got there as soon as she could. She was surprised to find how concerned she was. She almost got knocked over in the car park as she was so distracted. On entering the ward, she couldn't believe her eyes. Jane and Claire sat at his bedside. He was wired up to machines and looked deathly pale. His face was leaning to one side and he was dribbling. He couldn't speak. Standing in the room was a solicitor. He was frantically scribbling on a piece of paper as Jane shot her a filthy look.

'What's going on?' she asked.

'I am just making sure he has his wishes written down correctly.' Jane smiled.

The strength it took not to knock her out was incredible. Sammy felt her hackles rise and her jaw protrude. The adrenaline surged through her body and her heart rate soared. She wanted to grab that gold-digging piece of shit by the hair and punch her face in. This is what she had been waiting for. She had hung around like a foul smell, waiting for the day when he would be fragile enough to manipulate. Sammy looked at the solicitor. He looked embarrassed.

'You vulture,' she said and turned away. She had to leave. She was on the edge of losing all control.

Sammy knew there and then that she had been disinherited, and she knew that Jane had played the waiting game. She felt sick. In spite of everything they had gone through, she knew she loved him, and the thought of him dying was almost unbearable. She couldn't do anything about it. Jane was in control. There would be no Number Seven or Eight. She was it. She would be there till the death and inherit everything. There would be no more dinners. She had lost her father. It was only a matter of time, and she knew that Jane would not allow him to see her. She walked home, awaiting her fate. It wasn't long before she rang.

'Your father wants to go to the house in France to recuperate. Max and his wife are coming. He wants you to go. It's all arranged. Max will pick you up on Thursday morning. We will be away for ten days.'

Sammy was shocked. She had not been invited to his house in France before, and he had had it since 1997. She was pleased Max was driving; she wouldn't have coped in the same car as the gold-digger. They went by car and train. Claire and her friend were also in attendance. Her friend Debbie was the granddaughter of the former housekeeper. It was a right incestuous bunch. Sammy was treated like a child and given the same train cabin as the girls. They were twelve years old. There was a bar on the train and she went straight to it. The red wine soothed her frazzled nerves, and she steeled herself.

Jane stayed away from Sammy at the house. It was in the country with a pool, and the weather was good for the time of year. Her father looked very old and very frail. Jane stuck to him like glue, never letting them have any time together. She felt like a stranger, an unwanted guest. She remained quiet on holiday and read her book. It was a fascinating book on psychodynamic therapy, outlining how important the past was to the present. Sammy's past was so erratic and unstable that it was little wonder that she coped at all. As they sat by the pool, she heard Max say, 'What's it like to be the master of all you survey, William?'

Her father shot Sammy a look and replied to Max, 'Not quite all I survey, Max.'

The girls giggled with each other and played dressing up, hairdressers, and make-up artists. They invited Sammy to join them, but she couldn't. She had no wish to bond with them. One morning, she got up late, and her father seemed to have rallied round. He was cooking breakfast in the kitchen for everyone. She was the last to join them. He looked at her, and she thought she saw a glimmer of the old father she had known before his money and position had changed him for the worst. He seemed to be miles away and greeted her with a genuine smile.

'Morning, Sammy. Here's your breakfast.' He beamed at her as he handed her the plate, much to the disgust of Jane who had been waiting patiently for her food.

'Cheers, Dad. Thanks.' She smiled as Max pulled a face at her.

'Huh, you're still his favourite then, Sammy. We have all been waiting for ages!'

Jane's face was like thunder and Claire pouted.

'Fuck off, both of you!' she thought to herself.

The penultimate evening arrived, and Max and her father went to the local casino, leaving the women alone in the house. Sammy sat outside by the pool with Max's wife, Linda, and couldn't believe her ears when she overheard Claire telling Debbie that she had found her mom's vibrator and had tried it out. She even told her the colour. She was even more horrified when Debbie added that her mom had a purple one. What a delightful topic of conversation for twelve-year-olds.

Sammy opened a bottle of wine and they sat chatting. Linda made a massive effort to make Sammy feel welcome, but it was wasted. She was too deeply affected by all his marriages and relationships to respond or engage. She saw Jane pouring herself a Bacardi and coke and watched her knock it back. Half an hour later, she appeared outside and was noticeably drunk.

'Here we go,' Sammy mouthed to Linda.

'You nearly ruined your father, you ungrateful little bitch. You deserve nothing from him, nothing at all. I can't believe he bought that house and car after what you did. Your aunt is a money-grabber. I can see her mentally pricing up all his assets when she visits. You two will get nothing. No wonder you are like you are. Just look at your mother!' she goaded.

'Goodnight.' Sammy walked away. She knew better than to bite. It washed over her just like all of her predecessors.

Fortunately, Sammy shared Max and Linda's car on the return journey. After parking the car on the train, they were shown their cabins. Sammy had avoided Jane since her outburst and blanked her. Again, she had been put in the same cabin as the girls. They convened in the bar, and Sammy couldn't wait to get a glass of wine. The barman was giving her the eye, and she was glad of the distraction. He was cute, and she chatted and laughed with him for a good few hours. All the adults were drinking as they would be staying overnight on the train. The girls were in their cabin, which was situated next door to Max and Linda's. Sammy was invited back to the staff quarters with the barman, and in her fragile state, she couldn't wait to get out of Jane's company. She turned towards her father and said, 'Right, I am off for a shag. You don't mind, do you? Must run in the family, eh, Dad?'

Her father's mouth fell open and Jane stared at her.

'It's all down to my role model, William Davis. What an inspiration!'

She staggered towards the barman. Payback number two—how often had he completely ignored her for his love of sex?

'Sammy, come back here. You are supposed to look after the children!' Jane shouted.

'Fuck you and look after your own fucking kids! I am not a babysitter!' The barman laughed in awe and escorted her to the staff party.

Her head was throbbing in the morning. She woke up in a spare cabin and just about managed to find her way back to the bar in time to see Max and Linda. She was silent. As they boarded the ferry, she found a shop. Searching through the cards, she found a thank-you card and wrote in it:

'Dear Dad,

Thank you for the holiday, Sammy xx.'

Finding her father and Jane in the café, she went to hand him the card. Jane snatched it out of her hand and opened it. She mockingly read it out loud and looked at her. 'How cheesy!'

Sammy looked at her father, then back at Jane. 'She is not worth it, Sammy. She is trash, ignore her,' she told herself. Walking away, she vowed that one day she would slap her. She was relieved to get home and back to work. There was no word from her father again for weeks until he called her at home.

'I am getting married to Jane in June.'

'Well, thanks for telling me, Dad. You forgot to tell me the last time you got married to number four, you just showed me your ring after you did it. Best of luck to you. I won't be attending. I am busy that weekend, and besides, I have been to a couple of your weddings. Pencil me in for the next one, and I will see if I am free.' Payback number three—he hadn't attended her police passing-out parade. They were even. She waited for his response; he put the phone down. She had at least tried to repay his actions. He didn't handle them well. She wanted to mirror him to make him understand how it felt.

She heard nothing for months. She didn't attend the wedding. She avoided at all costs anything to do with him—local pubs, restaurants. She wanted to move; she wanted to be free from his legacy.

She decided to rent her house out privately. She found a tenant and let it out for six months. She moved away from the area and got a job as a security instructor; she rented a nice, new two-bedroom flat and started a new life.

Six months passed quickly, and she returned to her home town. She got in touch with old friends and went out drinking in town, she stupidly got in the car.

She sped along the dual carriageway driving way too fast. As she did so, her mobile rang, and she stupidly reached into her bag to answer it. She clipped the curb doing ninety miles an hour, and the car flipped over into a field. She felt it roll over and over and over again. She screamed out as the car came to a sudden stop when it hit a tree. She was upside down. Fortunately, she had her seatbelt on, and it had saved her life.

She tried to move and get out of the car, terrified that it would burst into flames. She screamed out in agony as her hands tried to undo the seat belt. She had broken her fingers in the steering wheel. She could feel the blood in her mouth and panicked.

'Are you all right? I have called an ambulance. Stay still, don't move. I am a police officer. You will be OK. Talk to me, try to stay conscious.'

She heard the sirens and heard voices, 'Jesus, is she alive?'

She felt the vibration on the door as the fire service cut through the twisted metal. A paramedic placed a mask over her mouth, and she passed out. She woke up in hospital. Her hands were in agony, she was strapped on to a stretcher with a collar on her neck, and she could taste blood.

'Sammy, you are very lucky to be alive. Is there anyone you want us to contact?' the nurse asked.

'Yes, my work colleague. I know the address not the phone number,' she replied.

'We will try and get a message to him for you. Now just relax. We need to check your spine. You may have a fracture. Your fingers on both hands are broken. You will have to go to the orthopaedic department for treatment.'

Two policemen and a doctor approached her and explained that they had suspected she was over the limit. She knew she was. She acknowledged her guilt and agreed to a blood test. She knew she would be banned again. She lay in the ward. Her body ached in pain as she realised just how lucky she was. There had been an off-duty police officer on his way to work driving behind her, and he had seen the car roll off the road. It had rolled seven or eight times before it struck the tree. If he hadn't seen it happen, she would have probably died in the field. The car was not visible from the road, and at that time in the early hours, there had been no one around. To her disbelief, her father walked in. He was dressed in a suit and looked furious.

'I suppose you were drunk!' he sneered at her.

She was still lying on a stretcher with a neck brace on. Her hands and arms were covered in bruises, her hair was full of dirt, leaves, and twigs, she had two black eyes, and she was bleeding.

'Remove me from your hospital details, Sammy. I don't want to be listed as your next of kin and once and for all, stay out of my life,' he said icily. The look in his eyes was one of pure malice.

'Have I made myself quite clear? Stay out of my life. I mean it. Goodbye and have a nice life!' She watched him walk away.

The first time they had laid eyes on each other was in a hospital thirty-seven years previously when she had been born. That moment he walked away was the last time they ever looked at each other. His hatred towards her was all-consuming.

CHAPTER SEVENTEEN

Moving On

She got her old job back. Her boss had an impossible crush on her, but she thought he was an idiot. She went straight back to work with her hands in bandages. She threw herself into it completely and decided never to look back. There was something seriously wrong with her father, and she was sick to death of being sucked in and pushed out on a whim. She was tired of it and had had enough. She would never forget how he had treated her. Of all the emotions she had ever felt, the pain from her father's rejection cut her to the core. People who didn't walk in her shoes offered all kinds of advice, but nobody could ever imagine how a parent's rejection made you feel unless they actually experienced it. Her life was extraordinary, and it hurt. She had tried her damned hardest to change the relationship. She had sacrificed herself for him, his business, and she had been treated like dirt. She swallowed hard and pushed it down again to the depths of her soul.

She met other instructors through her work and became aware of the next level of security, close protection—it was her next challenge. She needed to prove to herself that she could do it. She applied for her close protection course in Sussex and started to train in the gym. She figured it would be similar to her army training and knew that she could cope with the environment. She wanted to be able to travel with her work, and close protection offered her that opportunity. It would also offer her the opportunity to release her rage. There was plenty of it lurking beneath her calm exterior. To look at her, you would think that butter wouldn't melt, but she was seething.

She scrounged a lift to Sussex and booked into the hotel, the course was residential for a month. She would be staying at weekends too as she had no way of getting there and back. The delegates met in the bar on the Sunday evening before the course was due to start on the Monday morning. There were twenty-two of them and three instructors; she was the only female. During the course of the evening, they all chatted, and he discovered that all but one were ex-army. She felt like a square peg in a square hole. The alcohol flowed, and she enjoyed listening to war stories about Iraq and Afghanistan. She was in awe.

It transpired that there were several members of the Gurkha Regiment, the Paras, the Marines, the Royal Artillery, and the Naval Police. The instructors were former Special Air Services and Special Boat Services. Sammy felt slightly intimidated but kept her head high. She could do this. She was ex-Royal Military Police and ex-Civilian Police. This was her forte. Monday morning arrived, and she wished she hadn't drunk so much red wine. All the delegates sat in the classroom, waiting for the instructor. They were taught various subjects throughout the day, and she was introduced to another instructor who was a former Royal Protection Officer. He was comical and exceptionally proficient as an instructor.

She liked him, and he made the training fascinating by inserting real-life incidents into the curriculum. She understood how the training company had acquired the reputation for being the best in the world. The training was intense and ran normally from early in the morning to late in the evening. She was exhausted, but she loved it. Soldiers were a different type of animal. She really enjoyed their company.

The instructors were very knowledgeable, and she learnt many things from them. Krav Maga training was hard but nevertheless, she turned up in the gym for the training session. She knew many of the techniques as they were standard amongst police and prison officers. Every delegate was in turn thrown to the floor and put in excruciating arm and wrist locks. She had no ego to bruise but was covered in bruises by the end of the session.

The pace of the training was fast and furious. There was no room for slackers. It was the best of the best, and if you couldn't handle the pace, you would fall by the wayside. The hotel the delegates shared became almost like a barracks, and Sammy was filled with very fond memories from her teens. She regretted ever leaving her former careers. By the end of the second week, the class had tightly bonded and she had made good friends for life. The camaraderie and teamwork was something she had missed in her civilian career, where back-stabbing and one-upmanship had prevailed. The vast amounts of skills in the room were enviable, and everyone pitched in, creating an electric environment for learning. The course passed quickly, and they all met in a restaurant for their dining-in night. Sammy was so proud of herself—she had stayed the course. She had found her courage and her strength again. There would be no turning back. Doors were beginning to open for her again.

She returned from her training with a new-found confidence and a sense of pride. She immediately applied to her local college for a job and searched the security industry for avenues into her specialisation. It wasn't long before the college contacted her and she was offered a job as an instructor. She was also asked by the police to be a conflict management instructor for police community support officers. She had found her way back where she belonged. Going to work was a dream. She had never been so happy, and her students' praise of her teaching acumen made her beam with delight. She set up her own business and called it 'Bobbies'. She worked freelance with many training companies as an instructor and a consultant. She knew all the hard work had finally paid off. 'Bobbies' took off, and she gained an excellent reputation as an instructor. She made new friends teaching at the college and also undertook a university degree in teaching. Her life had begun again and it was almost like turning full circle.

In 2008, Sammy began to feel ill in the night with crippling stomach pains and vomiting. The doctor informed her she had gallstones and would need an operation. It was scheduled for May.

By all accounts, the operation went well, but two days later, she was in agony and was rushed back into hospital. She couldn't breathe, and the pain in her stomach was excruciating. She was given painkillers via a drip; she really believed that she was going to die.

The operation had failed and caused her lung to collapse. The surgeon also suspected that she had deep vein thrombosis. She was in a dangerous position, and was visibly shaken. Ten days passed as she laid in hospital, all her friends came to see her and she could tell by the look in their eyes that she was in a serious condition.

The Dr. said, 'I think I should let your next of kin know, you have no-one listed, whom shall I call?'

"Call my father." As the Dr returned, she could tell by his face that her father had refused to come.

She wondered if she would die and then thought that if she were to, then she would have to have liked to have said goodbye to her father and to have told him that despite everything, she loved him. She didn't get the opportunity.

CHAPTER EIGHTEEN

Bereavement

Sammy was released from hospital with a drain in her stomach to collect the bile. It was attached to a tube, then to a bottle that stuck out of her stomach. She had to carry it around with her for a week. She felt awful, and carrying the drain around with her was horrible. She was very down but relieved that she hadn't died. She received messages and cards from her work colleagues, friends, and students, and after a week of visits from the district nurse to clean and dress her wounds, she went back to have the drain removed.

The college would be closing for the summer, and she considered a career change. She browsed the web site and saw that an associate lecturer's position was available for the Higher National Certificate BTEC Diploma in Public Services. She applied for the position and attended the interview; she got the position and was due to start in September.

Sammy spent the summer maintaining her home. She extended the kitchen, the bathroom and decorated. She enjoyed DIY, and the house looked fresh and modern. She spent a fortune on the patio area, bushes, trees, and plants, and it was a pleasure to sit in during the summer evenings to study.

September soon came around, and she enthusiastically started her new job. She was teaching sixteen to nineteen-year-olds, and it was a challenge. She prepared her lessons and gave out her assignments on schedule. Marking them was very time consuming, and her Sundays were taken up with the task. Her subjects were uniformed public service, crime and effects, security, and custodial care. She knew her subject inside out and again excelled. She developed a good rapport with her students and tried to make the classes as interesting as possible. She drew on various techniques her past tutors had used in her training courses, and all in all, she was pleased with her performance. As September drew to a close, the weather changed and it became cold. She worried that her newly planted garden may not survive the approaching winter and missed the warm summer evenings spent in the garden.

October was dark and cold. On Sunday evening, she was running a bath when the doorbell rang. She answered it and was shocked to see her father's accountant standing in front of her. She knew instantly that there was something wrong.

'What's wrong? Has something happened to my father?'

'He died on Friday.' Replied the accountant.

Despite all the psychological abuse, the cruelty, and the rejection, Sammy reacted normally. Her father had treated her like a piece of dirt, he was on reflection a psychopath but she displayed completely normal grief reactions.

She went into shock and on to automatic pilot initially. She thanked the accountant for informing her and asked, 'What did he die of?'

'He had throat cancer and was very ill for six months,' the accountant replied.

'When is the funeral?' She was trembling.

'I will call you and let you know. I believe it will be the thirty-first of October, but I will confirm.'

'Halloween? Was he joking?' She thought.

'I will see you out.' She walked him to the door still in shock and then returned to the kitchen, her face contorted and the grief filled her entire body, the weight descended on her like a tonne of bricks as the pressure forced her to sit down, her only thought was,

'He should never have had children.'

The distress and relief came all at once. Her feelings were out of control, her mood swings frightened her. She had always hoped that there would be a reconciliation, that the relationship would change, that some miracle would happen, and he would be a father to her. Now it was final. There was nothing more she could do. His final rejection had come. He hadn't bothered to see her or attempt to make amends knowing he was dying. She should have expected it, but she was still devastated. She had no idea that he had been ill. If she had known, she would have gone to see him. He couldn't be a father. He didn't know how to be, but she had always been a daughter and she acted accordingly. It was natural and subconscious behaviour.

She drove to work the following morning and literally clung to the steering wheel to hold herself up. She thought she would collapse at any moment. She had a private word with her manager and told him she was OK. She made it through the morning, but as she sat in the office at lunchtime, the tears overwhelmed her and she couldn't face teaching. She told the manager she had to go and drove home. Burying her face into the cat's soft fur, she released her emotions and sobbed. She cried for her loss, what she had always wanted and never received from her father, and the reality that now it was never going to be possible. She cried for the little girl inside her that had lost everyone she had loved and the family that was taken from her.

Her house was still in trust. She was concerned now what would happen. Would she be thrown out? Was her life of instability about to return again?

Had he left it to her? She called the accountant and made an appointment to see him. 'What's going to happen to my home? Can I still live there?' she asked.

'I don't know yet. We have to see what his will states. I will send you a copy of the trust and the will when I have it.'

'I thought you were the trustee. Isn't it up to you what happens to the house now?'

The accountant shifted in his chair, and she knew he was lying. 'Like I said, I will have to wait until I have read the will,' he lied.

'Thanks, I want a copy of the trust right away. I need to be assured that I will not lose my home,' she told him.

She was getting nowhere and stood up. 'It's because I don't trust you. After what happened over the shares and America, do you blame me?' She walked out of his office.

She was now really worried. She had lived in her house for seven years and had made it her home. She had no idea what the future would hold for her now, and she couldn't afford anything as nice on her own income.

The funeral was held on Halloween. Sammy was appalled. Surely the arrangements could have been made for the day before or after. It seemed like another sick joke. As she entered the building, she was told that there was a separate room for family to wait in. As she approached the door, she was stopped by a complete stranger, certainly not a family member. The woman gave her a filthy look and said, 'This room is for family only. Who are you?'

Sammy said nothing and as she walked into the room, it turned silent. She vaguely recognised a couple of distant cousins but no one else. She saw the hearse arrive and her heart ached. As it approached the door, she saw to her disgust the flower arrangement on the top. It was a packet of cigarettes and a cigarette with a line of white smoke made of white and yellow flowers.

He had died of throat cancer; it was in very bad taste. She automatically walked out to meet the hearse. She didn't notice anything else. She had tunnel vision. She walked behind the coffin as the pole bearers carried it in. She was in shock and kept thinking, 'That's my father. Oh god, no. That's my father.' She held her tears in and kept her head up as the procession entered the room.

The pole bearers were the same group that had manhandled her out of her father's home years before, and she did her best to not make any eye contact with them. As she attempted to walk past them and on to a pew, they stood in her way. She was pushed back to the middle seats whilst members of staff and Number Six's family filled the front rows. She should have expected it. It all seemed so ridiculous. Her father was dead. Didn't anybody care how she felt? Whatever had she done to be treated so badly by his staff and his new family and friends? She didn't know, and now she would never know.

She sat as the eulogy began and felt her face turn red with embarrassment. 'William was married five times. Some of you may think it was six, but it was actually five as one was a common law wife,' the reader announced and then went on to mention all of the wives and children including her. 'He was worth about forty million and leaves behind his wife, Jane, and her daughter Claire, who will miss him dearly. He spent his last days at the casino and would like you all to now sing along to "I Did It My Way".'

Sammy nearly choked. She saw at the front of the room another flower arrangement—the king and queen of diamonds. She felt sick.

After the song, the sales manager from the company stood up and began his eulogy, 'The ladies at work used to love Thursday as William would come in with a bag of sweeties, and it was one sweet for a kiss, two sweets for a grope, and three, well, you can guess what he got for three!' She wanted the ground to swallow her whole. 'I also recall speaking to his secretary, and she told me how surprised she was to get the job. It all became clear when William told me it didn't matter about her qualifications. She had nice tits, ha, ha, ha!'

Sammy could not believe her ears. She wanted to walk out. She remembered why she had hated working for him. She remembered what a complete sexual pervert he was as she had never been so embarrassed in her life. The farce finally came to an end, and she walked straight out. She didn't stop to speak to anyone and got straight in the car and sped away her only thought 'Please don't ever let me be like them. Please don't let me be like him.'

Shock and denial hit her hard for the first few weeks; the funeral had been disgusting from start to finish. She was glad it was over. A copy of the will came in the post, and she read it in the kitchen, 'I leave my entire estate to my wife and stepdaughter and any children my stepdaughter may have. I leave nothing to Sammy as I have provided for her generously and finally during my lifetime.'

CHAPTER NINETEEN

Litigation

Sammy arrived at the solicitor's office and waited patiently. The managing partner introduced himself,

'Good morning. I am Liam. Can you tell me a bit about your situation?'

It took Sammy about two hours to reiterate the outline of her experience with her late father and the business. Liam looked visibly horrified as she told him the truth about the past. The first observation he made was that she had been ripped off when she sold her shares. She acknowledged that she had known that, but her circumstances were very different back then and she had been extremely ill and destitute. Liam thought she had a chance of recouping her losses under the doctrine of proprietary estoppel. Fortunately, he knew the solicitor who had handled her constructive dismissal case, and the files were found. Initial letters were sent to her trustees and her late father's solicitor, and litigation began. Sammy continued to work, but the strain began to show. She had no idea just how long it would be before she would have to leave her home, and it was making her ill. She crumbled in February in Dr. Hatton's office. Dr. Hatton had come to know Sammy well over the years, and he looked deeply sad for her.

'Did you really believe he would leave you anything, Sammy, after all he did to you?' he asked tentatively.

'Yes, I always hoped he would. I know I am a fool, but I can't help how I feel. I can't hate him. He was my father. You wouldn't understand.'

'Your results show that you are severely depressed, Sammy, and I don't want you relapsing at all. I want you to take Prozac and come and see me every month. Do you feel like killing yourself?' He was the only person to ever ask her. She was relieved and shocked to hear it. So many people couldn't ask that question.

'Yes, I do. My parents hate me; my brother must have hated me too. It's my entire fault. I am such a terrible person.' The tears poured down her face and she couldn't breathe. She gasped for air, sobbing as she collapsed forward on to his desk.

'Take some time off work. I will get you some counselling urgently. Promise me you will go."

'Yes. I will go. Thanks,' she sniffed.

Passing her a tissue, he smiled gently and said, 'You will get through this, Sammy. Everyone is on your side, you know. Your father's behavior has disgusted the whole town. You are grieving, give it time, it will pass.'

Sammy got her prescription and drove home. She went to bed. Half term was approaching and there was little news from her solicitor. Documents and wills were being scrutinised, and she dreaded the monthly invoices that she was receiving. She couldn't afford the cost. She was broke. Desperate, she approached the bank and managed to get a small loan. A meeting with a prominent barrister was arranged, and she met him and Liam in his office.

'We have made some progress, Sammy. Your father has made twenty wills in the last ten years. You are in most of them up until he married his latest wife. His employees were too, but it appears that since his marriage to her, she and her daughter are now his only beneficiaries. His estate has been valued at forty-two million pounds.'

Sammy wasn't in the least surprised. 'What about my house? Do I have to leave?'

'We will write to the trustees and ask them what their position is. There is some good news. As you were being supported by him when he died, you have a claim on his estate. We also want to meet with a Queen's Counsel as we think there may be a case for you to have your shares returned. The circumstances under which they were sold are disgraceful, and it should never have happened. You were too ill to know what you were doing, and it all took place under huge duress,' the barrister added.

'I don't have enough money to do this. I am now off sick from work. I am severely depressed.' She was morose.

'I can see no reason why this can't be done on a conditional fee agreement, no win, no fee. We will draw one up for you, but if you do win, we uplift our charges by 75 per cent. You can claim most of this back off the defendant afterwards.' The barrister smiled.

'That's great! When are we going to see the Queen's Counsel? I am available anytime now, really, as I am not working.' She brightened up.

'I will be in touch, Sammy. We are just going to discuss matters further now, so I will see you out,' Liam replied, showing her out.

In early May, the agreement was drawn up and signed. A flurry of emails and letters were exchanged between parties. Sammy's mental health deteriorated and she became withdrawn. She had to relive her past in great detail. It cut her to pieces again as if the wounds were recently inflicted. She met with her Queen's Counsel in June and cried during the meeting. The Queens Counsel was empathetic and passed her a tissue, but the situation was slowly triggering her post-traumatic stress, and Sammy knew she was falling again. She was suffering from PTSD and was experiencing flashbacks, nightmares, and homicidal thoughts towards Number Six and Claire. She was jealous, jealous that they had had the love that she had wanted, jealous that he had loved them and not her, jealous that they would possibly inherit what had destroyed her life, her family, and her relationship with her father for nothing. Neither had worked there. They had just spent the profits without a thought about anyone else but themselves.

Sammy raged silently. Her solicitor sent her Number Six's response to her letter of claim. She had totally rejected it, alleging outrageous lies against Sammy. Sammy read the response and was shocked to see that Number Six had stated that Sammy had been dismissed from the police for misconduct and had not left at her father's request. She stated that Sammy had also broken into her father's home and business. She also slandered her, saying that she was a drug addict and an alcoholic and couldn't be trusted to handle money. Sammy laughed at her stupidity. Did she not understand that she had to prove these allegations? It wasn't possible as they were total fabrication. With her rejection letter, she attached a letter-headed typed letter from her father to the police. It was dated before his heart attack and stroke and was an instruction to the staff to escort Sammy off the business premises and for the police to arrest her and charge her for trespass. Sammy laughed out loud. Number Six obviously was stupid. Trespass was a civil offence, and the police would not arrest her and couldn't charge her with it. The very fact that she has been on holiday with them after the letter was typed was hilarious. She thought that any police officer in their right mind would have laughed at her, and it would have been a great joke at the station. Sammy concluded that Jane's only talent must have been opening her legs for a dirty old pervert.

Her legal team had a chuckle over the letter as they produced the evidence to totally disprove her lies. Sammy's police personnel file was produced that specifically stated that her father had been ill and asked her to join the family business. It also stated that she had an exemplary record and would be a loss to the force. Sammy had no criminal record, so the allegations of burglary and trespass were disproved. Number Six was obviously trying to slander Sammy and had tried her hardest to justify the abhorrent treatment. Sammy decided to pay her back and telephoned the *Daily Mail.* The reporter went to her late father's house and confronted Number Six. He telephoned Sammy when he got back and told her that she had told him to get off her property, yelling, 'If you write anything about me, I will sue the arse off you!' Sammy laughed out loud. The article ran, and the headline said it all: 'Millionaire leaves fortune to sixth wife thirty-one years his junior'. Sammy and her friends read it at the local bar and all laughed. 'Fuck you! You gold-digging bitch!' they toasted.

Sammy was touched by the empathy around her. People came out of the woodwork to support her and make statements. Max's statement was enlightening. He told the solicitor that her father had been seeing other women all through his last marriage and entertained sex workers for oral sex as it was something that Jane wouldn't do. He also stated that Jane had a new lover who had attended the funeral and the scattering of the ashes. He had apparently moved in with her, and plans were being made to demolish the house and build a new one. Sammy was not surprised as she had sussed Number Six out on sight. Her fathers' friends stated that they had begged her late father to get in touch with Sammy and make his peace. But they were convinced that Number Six would not let him and was manipulating and controlling him from the day he had his stroke and heart attack.

Former members of staff and suppliers came forward to make statements in Sammy's favour, and they all expressed how disgusting they thought the funeral was. Number Six's name was mud. She no longer had her husband to hide behind. The gloves were off, and Sammy played to win. She may have lost a battle in the past, but she would win the war. She was as intelligent as her father and had played games with him and his wives all her life. She had become more than adept.

Her trustees hid behind a wall of silence, and the Queen's Counsel told her that they would bring proceedings against them if they attempted to remove her from her home.

A forensic accountant was instructed and demanded the company's accounts, articles of association, and sale transfers. Paperwork that Sammy had not seen from the tribunal came to light and reading it through was enlightening. Her post-traumatic stress was triggered, but she fought it off and managed to write a very detailed report of what had happened and pulled Janes defence to pieces. It seemed obvious that her father had paid everyone off to lie for him. It was a typical modus operandi for him. In her absence from the company in 1997, he had illegally removed her as a shareholder, a director, and a trustee of the pension fund. Her signature had been forged, and the letters were typed by Mrs Jones. Her father had also acquired a loan in her name as joint director for half a million pounds from the NatWest Bank. Again, her signature had been forged. She stared in disbelief at her forged signature and called the economic fraud unit to report it. No wonder he had left her for dead. He had dismissed her as easily as the rest of his unfortunate close family. He was ruthless.

The evidence was collated diligently. It took nearly two years for her and her legal team to piece together the whole factual matrix. It was unreal. Sammy used her latent detective skills, and the team were thrilled that she could make such an exacting witness statement. She recalled everything but it was traumatic. The triggers had all been pulled again, and she looked homicidal. It was a good thing that her father was dead. She would have murdered him.

She became fixated firmly concluding that her father was a sociopath. There was nothing wrong with her that couldn't be fixed with time and love. She just had to get over this last hurdle, and her father and his disgraceful associates would never be able to harm her again. It took all of her strength not to confront Jane and the cronies at the company and vent her rage.

As part of their evidence, Sammy had to see a leading psychiatrist in suicide and self-harm; she was nervous about the meeting. Prior to her appointment, the psychiatrist had a copy of her entire medical records, which were punctuated with counselling and episodes of depression.

In the meeting she was questioned about her history and she didn't hold back. If she was insane, then she would have welcomed being taken into care. She didn't have the strength to deny or fight what was happening to her psyche. The meeting lasted an hour and she was unemotional. She had flicked the switch and was running on autopilot. The report was sent to her a month later and she read it eagerly. The psychiatrist who had written the report for the purpose of the court had summarised his findings:

In my opinion, on the balance of probabilities, she lacked capacity during 1996. The extent of this impairment of capacity is likely to have varied with her mental state, possibly from week to week (or faster). I consider that there must be serious doubt as to whether she had full capacity to make decisions such as the sale of the shares in the autumn 1997 period.

Further, it seems likely that her dispute with her father was affecting her mental state (and in reverse, the relationship was affected by her mental state). She appeared to be well on 21 December 1997 as a result of an apparent resolution of her problems. In my opinion, on the balance of probabilities, she was influenced by anxiety and depression during the run-up to this settlement, and that she was frankly disinhibited or psychotic during the middle part of 1997 whilst in the USA and for some parts of 1996.

Indeed, in the weeks prior to my interview, she had been referred to the Crisis Resolution and Home Treatment Team because of concerns about her deteriorating mental state. In my opinion, it is unlikely that she will be able to hold down long-term employment. This opinion is based on the unpredictability of her illness, tendency to relapse when under stress in recent years, and her general past employment history. I note comments in the General Practice notes that she had applied successfully for a number of jobs but had rarely been able to stay in them for longer than a few weeks. I note that up to 2008, she had worked as a part-time lecturer. However, it is not clear how successful this was. It was part-time and she ultimately gave up.

In my opinion, on the balance of probabilities, she is unable to work for more than minimal remuneration in the future because of her recurrent psychiatric problems.

Although it is ultimately a matter for the court, it is my opinion that Sammy, through no fault of her own, is psychologically vulnerable and dependent upon others. In the recent past, it is clear that she was heavily dependent upon her father for income. Paradoxically, she was also dependent on her father for emotional support (whether received or not). This was support which often was not forthcoming or was negative. It is my opinion that Sammy would qualify for being disabled under the Disability Discrimination Act. In the context of her psychological vulnerability, she appears to have a claim on her father's estate as a dependent.'

Sammy was vindicated; she had longed to hear the words, 'through no fault of her own'. That was what she had been fighting for, not financial gain, just vindication, and this report meant she had a claim; she took a sharp intake of breath.

She had what she needed to retrieve her self-esteem and to go to court; the defendants were hammered with witness statements, company reports, and medical evidence. Sammy couldn't wait to go to trial. The defendants backed down and asked for a quick mediation. In November 2010, she attended the mediation, and as she walked into the room, Number Six was already seated with her legal team. Sammy held her head high and looked straight through her. Coming this far was already a victory for her. It wasn't about the money; it was principle.

The mediator opened the discussion, and the first objection Number Six had was the cost of Sammy's legal team. Sammy raised her eyebrows. Money was the only thing on Number Six's mind. There she sat with the possibility of inheriting forty million pounds, whilst denying Sammy anything, not even the roof over her head, and she had to quibble about money.

'Don't look at her and don't say anything,' Liam instructed as her Queen's Counsel set out her case. They then went into separate rooms as the mediator conducted shuttle diplomacy, attempting to come to a settlement figure. Both sides locked horns and mediation was unsuccessful. It had been a long day, and Sammy was exhausted. It had taken twenty-six months to come to this point, and it had dragged her to hell and back. She saw Number Six walk past the window and looked at her; she felt nothing at all.

Liam contacted her at home, and figures were banded about. They finally came up with a settlement figure both parties agreed on, and the relevant documents were signed just before the New Year. It was finally over, and Sammy could move away and start again.

Chapter Twenty

Therapeutic Change

At the end of January she relocated, she rented the house and moved. She couldn't wait to get out of the town; she had truly been tried to her limit. Sammy started new life miles away in a new country near the beach. The relief was enormous. She never had to think or speak about her past again. No one knew her there, and she didn't need to feel ashamed or embarrassed any longer. She made her last will and testament leaving her estate to The Royal Society for the Prevention of Cruelty to Children. She changed her appearance, her name, and bought a new car.

A distant look descended over her eyes as she picked her handbag up, her usual bright blue eyes had turned cold. Sammy smiled as she felt for the hammer in her bag and drove to her late father's home. She would make sure her wish succeeded, not her fathers.

Number Six opened the door. Sammy swung the hammer high.

Epilogue

The final chapter in the book is not true. It is a depiction of what Sammy wanted to do when her PTSD took over; fortunately, she had a wealth of psychological support and has been counselled in anger management.

www.ingramcontent.com/pod-product-compliance
Lightning Source LLC
Chambersburg PA
CBHW030755200726
48288CB00004B/1185